soft dim skies

soft dim skies

a story of titan

simon petrie

Typeset in Adobe Garamond Pro / Candara
Cover illustration by Peter Jurik / Shutterstock

National Library of Australia Cataloguing-in-Publication entry

Title: Soft Dim Skies: a story of Titan / Simon Petrie.
ISBN: 9780648383659 (pbk.)
Subjects: Science fiction, Australian.
Other Authors / Contributors:
                Morrison, James, editor.
                Jurik, Peter, cover art.
Dewey Number: A823.4

books by simon petrie

(the titan sequence)

Matters Arising from the Identification of the Body

Wide Brown Land

Soft Dim Skies

Flight 404

Murder on the Zenith Express: the Gordon Mamon collection

80,000 Totally Secure Passwords That No Hacker Would Ever Guess

Tremendously Inconveniencing A Great Many Photons

The 1001 Top Immortality Treatments You Must Try Before You Die

introduction

One morning in late 2008, I woke early and, having assessed that 'sleep mode' was temporarily inaccessible, I rose and went downstairs. It was during that odd patch on the calendar between Christmas and New Year, when for most people the old year has finished, the new one hasn't started, and the day of the month ceases to carry any significance. We were staying down the coast (by which I mean the South Coast of New South Wales, which is neither particularly south nor particularly new, but that's a quibble for another time) in a unit we'd booked for several days away from the city.

That morning, I started work on a story, or at least on something which might turn into a story: I often start things without having any idea where they will lead. Often they don't lead anywhere; or if they do end up leading into something which can ultimately be called a story, this may not happen for several years. On this occasion, though, it only took a few months before I was sufficiently content with the story to send it out into the world. I submitted it to *Aurealis*, the longstanding Australian SF magazine which had only recently accepted an earlier story of mine, 'Latency'; they accepted this one too. This was my first story set on Titan, 'Storm in a T-Suit'. (I was, probably wisely, advised off my initial proposed title for the story, 'Shitstorm'.) Setting a story on Titan was an important moment for me: I had been fascinated with Titan (or more particularly with Titan's atmosphere, because one of the things which sets it apart as a moon is that it has one) for a couple of decades by this point, since the days of my PhD research. I'd written a few academic papers concerning details of its upper-atmosphere chemistry; now I had a story set on its surface.

'Storm in a T-Suit' was published in *Aurealis* vol. 44 (their twentieth anniversary issue) in August 2010. It might well have ended there, because I often don't re-use story settings, but Titan had its hooks in me: now there was another idea I'd conceived, a clear and classic idea which centred on Titan's characteristics but which at that time I could not directly connect, try as I might, with the plot for any possible story.

To put it baldly, I wasn't ready to write the thing.

So I wrote around it. I knew for this concept that I would need characters other than just those in 'Storm'; I concocted these characters, gave them their own stories. Often these stories were as much about exploring the setting of Titan, and of its unique combination of extreme cold and vaguely Earthlike features—streams, seas, rain, sand dunes, atmospheric haze and so on—as they were about the characters' glimpsed lives, though I have consistently tried to make those glimpsed lives interesting in their own right. Along the way, I populated Titan, gave it settlements and industries and struggles and reasons for habitation. I tried always to play fair by Titan, to describe the natural environment with reasonable accuracy; this hasn't been straightforward, because there is still so much unknown about that haze-shrouded world. It's possible that this incompleteness of available knowledge, this still-pixellated vagueness in our understanding of Titan is a part of what has kept me intrigued by it: where there is uncertainty, there is mystery; where there is mystery, there may be intrigue; where there is intrigue, there might be stories.

Eventually, there were enough such stories, enough such characters, for a book of my stories set on Titan: *Wide Brown Land*. Most of those short stories don't connect with each other, except through the overall setting; at least, that's how I imagine it appears to readers, because some of the connections, concerned with that central, clear idea which I hadn't managed to actuate in any story, simply do not show.

This novella, I hope, may change that. It draws together characters and story elements from most of the *Wide Brown Land* stories, in ways I had long intended. That said, those earlier stories are not 'required reading' for this novella (though naturally I'd be delighted if you went back to explore them later; conversely, I would be thrilled to bits if you *have* read the earlier stories and picked this book up primarily because of its oppotunity to further explore my vision of Titan's habitation).

Anyway, enough preamble. Please turn the page, and find yourself on Titan. Dress warmly.

Simon Petrie
March 2023

one

She was late. Which did nothing—or, at least, nothing constructive—for Cory's unease. He was tempted to just get up, to leave before her eventual arrival. But that, of course, would be too much the statement from him: both in public, here, now, amongst the restaurant's congregation of strangers; and more personally, to her, for whom he still cared in a way he knew she would not; a way she did not herself welcome.

It was difficult.

It had been difficult ever since.

He found himself semi-consciously curtailing the thought. To follow that idea, that knot of emotion and memory, was to lose himself in a past so hard-edged and acutely angular that he could not help but damage himself anew against its surfaces; and he would not put himself—and, by the osmosis of interpersonal perception, put her—through that anew. It had been a difficult skill for him to learn, but the learning had been needful. He would be careful around the things which caused him pain, amidst which the sight of her was central.

Around him, a hubbub of conversation. Shop talk between culturefarmers, geochem prospectors, polymer engineers; gossip between admin functionaries and delegates from the big convention currently straining the settlement's reserves of accommodation, produce, and breathable air; the playful hierarchical dialogues of families choosing to take some public rec time; earnest, soft-voiced, sometimes urgent communications between lovers at one of the vaguely signposted intersections on the journey to, or from, intimacy. An unexceptional Thursday in Levin, in other words.

But she was late, and Cory didn't know how much more endurance there was left in him. He found himself dwelling—despite his vow—on what or who might be behind the delay in her arrival. Laith, most probably; she had let slip a remark or two, when last he'd spoken to her, that suggested a physicality to her new relationship of which he did not think he could ever not be jealous.

The sharp angles of the past: this was what made unbearable the present.

But there she was, and she was smiling.

He would need to smile too.

They got the small talk out of the way with an enviable efficiency. In truth, there wasn't much of that, anyway: she would conceal from him the things she knew, or suspected, would cause him pain (in that sense, her mention of Laith, a month previously, had been a slip on her part). And since there was little he could share that would not sound unbearably dull against the reports of her progress at work, he largely didn't. It was obvious, from her demeanour, that chatter was not her goal for the evening. He was supremely uncomfortable with speculating what that goal might be: the possibilities included pain, the re-abrasion of wounds imperfectly healed. He'd mask that, of course; but the mask pinched. He expected she knew that.

The large talk wasn't what he'd been anticipating. Not that he was sure, at all, what that had been; but it had not been this.

She did most of the talking. Cory did not, in fact, know how to respond to her; could see that some mode of response was required, but failed in the delivery, focussed instead on a meal for which he'd lost a large portion of his appetite.

'Please say something,' she said, once her explanation was done.

That face: the careful smile, the eyes intense, thick messy hair. Recent cryo scarring on her cheek, an asymmetry she did nothing to disguise. Her fragrance; and he wasn't, at all, the sort to notice a woman's scent, but hers was somehow a signature: not cursive, not floral, not properly legible, subtle yet unmistakeable. The shallow rise and fall of her breathing. Each component was resonant, with his memory and with the many-edged difficulty he experienced in her presence. His autonomous functions demanded continuing attention; so also the need not to blush, while he did not properly understand why he should be drawn towards blushing; he was acutely conscious, too, of his facial muscles, which refused to ease. Her, waiting. Some moments were quiet, incipiently chaotic, potentially devastating. He honestly did not know which words he dare employ.

'When will you be back?' he asked, in just that tone. After too long a pause.

'I maybe won't,' she replied.

He kept going.

Financially, this meant coding piecework; short-run custom engineering printoffs, gear that fitted a particular need, but not one broad enough for the big industry players to have bothered with; and sundry field maintenance call-outs. Someone needed a replacement heating jacket for a condensibles monitoring rig, someone else was looking to coax a warranty-expired component into continuing operation, a third person didn't trust the autocalibration programming on an airqual gauge and wanted it checked. The work was varied, and tolerably challenging. In other respects, he sleepwalked, registering only in rearview that an event had occurred; that he was hungry; that it was time for sleep. He felt both peeled raw and numb. An exhausted insomniac. An unconscious nerve-bundle.

The engineering work, and the rest, kept him fed and housed, but barely. Plus it was erratic, some daycycles rushed, some entire weeks fallow. He was good, though, at what he took on, was dependable for most assignments, and nodded politely when clients told him—as more than one did—the trade was such that he would do well at it, on a financial basis, once he'd made a name for himself within the settlement.

He did not care to make a name for himself. Did not care, and did not dare. To make a name would be to invite problematic attention. His existence was best seen as something interstitial, for the next few years at least. Once sufficient time had passed, though, things should go more easily.

It turned out he was wrong about that.

The client was one he knew; or rather, one with whom he'd dealt before. They had asked for some programming, unexceptional assignments that drew on his strengths in coding and quasi-autonomous intellect interfacing, and they'd paid in full on each occasion, and always without the necessity of any reminder. This was an endearing trait in a client, and Cory added them to his 'approved' list. But the latest request was different: not just licence-skirting patchware this time; there was an engineering component to it too. Truth to tell, Cory wasn't convinced he was up to it; nor were they offering top credit for the task.

He figured it would be best to explain his reservations upfront, salvage the opportunity for further work from them even if it meant they had to ask elsewhere this one time.

Cory's previous work for the client had been via code-bundle drops on the mesh; he reckoned this latest task, involving most likely his polite refusal on a job that wasn't really an ideal fit for his skills, could also be done without requiring a complete face-to-face. Avatar-level should suffice. This, too, was a level of his survival strategy: do not stand out, do not attend in person, do not allow too many people to put a face to the carefully chosen name. Do not invite unnecessary trouble.

He briefed the avatar, which wasn't, all up, a demanding effort: his avatar had handled similar matters before, though as always the particulars were different. Then, satisfied that it could negotiate the conversation, he allowed connection.

The client didn't.

Two minutes later, an alert on his messaging implant: *Can we meet? S.*

He wished not to. But work was work, even the offer of unsuitable work which would, therefore, require to be declined. *Very well. Sometime this afternoon? My current personal is 1:32 p.*

Close enough, the client responded. *Busy for the next few. But I can do seven.*

Which, clearly, was late as work-time went, but it wasn't an issue. Irregular hours were a stock-in-trade. Where should we meet? He'd just need to remember a meal first.

Except, as it turned out, there wouldn't be a need to remember that. The client, this mysterious Snead, had arranged to meet him at a restaurant.

It was only after confirming this that he realised. The establishment, now under a new name, was the same restaurant where he and Arum had last met, where she had delivered her bombshell about fleeing offworld.

His thoughts, those next few hours, were more difficult than was standard.

Punctuality is a virtue in business, so he was early. The restaurant's name might have changed, but it appeared nothing else had. He explained to the check-in system that he was here as the guest of Snead, was instructed to wait (for no clear purpose, since there were tables of differing sizes visibly free) and, after a few minutes, was directed to the flagged table. Alcoved. He hoped that wasn't going to be an add-on.

Snead, it transpired, was a woman.

He stood, offered his hand, his forename. They shook. 'Portia,' she informed him. Her grip on his hand was sure, but lacked the bone-crimping roughness of some clients.

She was tall and, he surmised, several years older than him. Perhaps a decade. She seemed not so much to view his face as to read it. It was an uncomfortable thought.

It was made more uncomfortable by the realisation that her perfume was a close match for Arum's. Not that this Portia could ever be mistaken for his former lover; but it augmented his lack of ease.

Brass tacks, he told himself. 'It's an interesting job you've offered me, but I don't think I can help you.' He managed to avoid stumbling over the words' delivery.

'That's a pity,' she replied, and there was something in her pronunciation of those words which hinted at a dialect he couldn't pin down. 'I really need this to pass through as few hands as possible, and yours were recommended to me.'

'May I ask by who?'

'By whom,' she responded. 'Of course you may.' She perused the menu, made her selection. 'By someone you've known a long time.'

Which was not an encouraging thought, given that a primary focus for him had been the leaving behind of a substantial inventory of personal history. Crimes. Poor choices. Deaths, one of which had so nearly been his. He tried to formulate who, among his circle of longstanding friends, would know where to find him. There was, really, only the one: and she was far-flung by now, if her declaration that night had been in any way reliable.

He could not ask further. It was, somehow, too pointed a topic. But he also could not simply let the matter slide. Logging his own choice of meal, he asked, 'You're looking at mobile stream flow monitoring?'

'I'm looking at getting some mobile stream flow monitors adapted,' she replied.

'To what end?'

'You just said you didn't think you could help.'

'I quite possibly can't. But if I had a clearer sense of what you were hoping to achieve, I may be able to come up with a workaround.'

'I'm going to need something a bit more reliable than a workaround,' she said.

Not from here, not with that accent. Not from Levin, nor any of the surrounding minor settlements dotted around the uplands lying north of the Belet dunefields. And not from Ponnamperuna, which had been

Cory's home, prior to the attempted CREVjacking and its shambolic, mortal aftermath; nor Niemann; nor, he fancied, from anywhere across the northern farside. And yet the task was a reasonable-sounding one, given the locale: the topography around Levin was right for runoff, with tracks often cut by deluge-fed liquidways. If it was indeed stream flow monitoring which this Portia was intending, which he didn't believe it was. This didn't really concern him: but it was a simpler problem, one seemingly more amenable to constructive analysis, than the one which did. Namely, that she somehow knew him, or at least knew *of* him, through some connection she had chosen not to divulge. It was concerning, especially in view of the efforts he had made, in moving here, towards inconspicuousness.

Her self-evident confidence suggested he could trust her. Her evasiveness suggested otherwise.

He needed more data.

'You're not being very specific,' he said. 'In my experience, job fulfilment is generally most satisfactory when clear guidelines are given. You won't tell me what it is you want to achieve, nor will you tell me who recommended me to you.' *Let alone how you found me here, under a changed family name*, he thought, though of course could not say this. 'It's hardly surprising that I'm left with the impression I can't provide meaningful assistance to you. It's not really a way to do business, I have to say.'

'I knew your aunt,' she told him, steadily meeting his gaze. 'She spoke of you as highly capable, and methodical, and inventive. All of which are qualities I can use on this project.'

'Which is? Stream flow monitors are mature tech nowadays, you don't require someone to craft custom mods into them if you're using them for their stated purpose.'

'You're right,' she replied. 'It's adaptation towards a non-standard end. I can't really say more than that. I need someone I can trust. Until I know that person is you, I can't be completely specific. But from what I heard from Teresa Maria, you appear a good fit. And your work has been good to this point.'

The food arrived. They made a start.

'The payoff is not exactly high,' he complained. *I need to keep my nose clean, can't be seen to be involved in anything unlawful. And this whole setup—*

'The rate is what it is, unfortunately. Half upfront, half on completion.' She looked away for a few moments. 'It's possible there'll be a completion bonus, depending on the outcome.'

The penny dropped. 'You're looking for something,' he said.

'Yes,' she said.

'I still don't know that I can help,' he replied. 'The mods you're asking for, they're fine, nothing I can't handle, but the build is quite involved. I'd have to check a few options, refresh my technique, and even so I'd be lying if I said I was sure I could handle it. Not sure who could, actually, not round here.'

'Your work has been good so far.'

'Thank you.' He waited, hoping she would follow his hint towards seeking help elsewhere, but she did not. The silence extended.

Why did she not want to take the task to someone else? True, there would not be many in a settlement the size of Levin with the experience to perform the build satisfactorily, but that didn't explain her expectation that he would just take it on. There was something else there, undisclosed.

He could fuss about the whys and wherefores, but that wouldn't meet living expenses. And she wouldn't be paying him to second-guess, except in the context of troubleshooting the ware.

'Look, leave it with me for a couple of cycles,' he said at last. 'I'll get back to you with an answer.'

'I'd appreciate if you could give a response by noon tomorrow,' she said.

It was pressure he didn't need, but work was work.

He'd figured it out. Nonlocal; secretive; driven; ostensibly above board. Assuming she was genuine, assuming she was not implicit in an illegal activity of some form—or at least nothing more illegal than seeking to prolong equipment lifetimes beyond their manufacturer-mandated expiry dates, and pretty much everyone dabbled in that activity, even, or so he'd heard, the local pol—then she had to be a prospector, and the most likely explanation was that she was prospecting for heavy.

If it were so, then the half-payment upfront wasn't especially attractive. Ore-hunting on Titan was a dupe's game, especially nowadays when most of the most obviously promising locations had been exploited. The sites which remained seldom yielded anything of value, or so he'd gathered. But prospectors generally had a look about them, a sense of poker-faced desperation crossed with cunning, and she didn't have that. Appeared, all in all, to be both too materially well-to-do and too… not exactly too educated, although plainly she was highly trained in some field, but rather too at ease with society to be a prospector. Or to be a seasoned prospector, at any rate. Maybe she was a couple of busted digs away from such a state. Which, all in all, made this a bad assignment. It'd be best if his answer was no.

His answer was yes. An upcoming client cancelled at the start of the next cycle, and his roster was suddenly more barren than it had been for a long time. It was the work which Portia was offering—which he wasn't sure he could fully deliver, and for which he'd receive barely adequate compensation, even assuming she paid the balance on completion, which seemed questionable—or it was nothing.

Seventy percent upfront, he informed her, wondering what recourse he'd have if she didn't agree. Hardball wasn't his style.

Fortunately, she accepted his terms.

It took him a standard week, dawn to dusk of a slow Titan day, before he was able to see progress in the task. He'd chosen to pursue the more difficult aspect first, the build, because that was what made sense, even if the modding would have yielded a better failure-to-complete part-payment if he'd had to cancel for something more urgent, more achievable, more in line with his skills set. No such orders came in, however: it was Snead's work or nothing.

The first print was a disaster, fried before it had even had a chance to anneal: ten hours wasted. He spent a day redesigning, ferreting out those corners he'd improperly cut on the first attempt, bulking out the design for the casing, adding redundancy. As a result, the second effort was better, but didn't function: this, he thought, after scoping and re-checking every step of the design, was because her requested operating specs were off. He contacted her to report this, asked her—in perfect politeness, he had thought—to please re-evaluate her power-use requirements, because to his mind they seemed excessive; was surprised at her curt, almost angry rebuttal. It wasn't his place to question her specs, or her competence; she had scrupulously calibrated the details of the device's required operation before she had approached him to construct and equip it; she was regretting having agreed to the seventy percent. She knew what was needed from the equipment, and he did not; she did not need his technical second-guesswork, except in regard to details of the customisation which allowed him to realise what she was asking of him. He apologised, not knowing entirely why he did so, and redid his design. Still he was sure her specs were off; but he kept his ongoing suspicions private.

The third attempt almost worked, almost performed as she required. The fourth failed, because of a stupid and fully avoidable mistake on his part, and that day he resolved to finish early so as not to compound matters. The fifth iteration was a twenty-hour print—the longest yet—which wrecked his sleep for the next night and his appetite for the next day.

It worked.

It worked in the workshop, but he was fairly sure it would fail in the field, within weeks of deployment. Arguably, this wasn't his concern, but the harm to his reputation was something it would be better to avoid. He re-engineered the problem, retaining only the best components of the previous design and simplifying a large section of the drive mechanism, imprecating as he did so against clients left carefully unnamed. The sixth print was what was required, exactly. Or almost exactly, at least, and the necessary refinements could be included, he thought, as add-ons to the working prototype rather than needing to be crafted afresh from whole cloth. Now he could mod, and soon he could deliver. And could seek the next assignment.

*

There were seven weeks of piecework, after this, for other clients: life-support-system custom mods for a vehicle with refurbished cyclers; jailbreaking a survey scope so as to avoid providing manufacturer access to the captured imagery; debugging a third-party licence for a reinitialised T-suit's reactive acoustics. And more of the same. Typical Levin jobs, seeking for the most part to maintain functionality that already existed, or to restore, rather than to create anew. Maintenance, he thought, was probably what he was best at. The tasks were seldom truly interesting, but they were varied enough, and they kept him in credit, more or less. He began to think he'd seen the last of the Snead work: not that this bothered him, exactly, but the suspicion that he might have somehow driven off one of his more dependable clients, either through the time taken to reach success with the build or through his perceived criticism of her still-unspecified competence, would not die completely.

There followed a fallow week, and more than a week, with nothing to do except watch his balance dwindle. He took an approach which carried some risk, and which went against his ambitions towards a maximally unobtrusive existence: he contacted those of his client base for whom he had performed a minimum of three completed tasks during his time in Levin, to state his availability for further work, currently, should they have it. It wasn't a long list; and he didn't include Portia Snead among the recipients, though she qualified according to the criteria he'd set himself. There had just been something about that last assignment which rubbed him wrong.

As it happened, though, his next task came from her, rather than from any of those he'd sought out. Well, it would keep him afloat.

Nighttime—by which he meant genuine night, the long week-plus of darkness, rather than his own personal time of slumber and reprieve from labour as allotted by the clock-face—nighttime was difficult for Cory. It mattered nothing that the light levels within the corridors and atria and chambers of Levin's commercial and recreational district were as high at this time as they were during the sunlit hours, nor that those byways were, if anything, more busy during that dark week. Nor did the burnt-metal stink of tholin in the corridor adjoining the settlement's main industrial airlock change perceptibly from Titan day to Titan night, nor the settlement's temperature, nor the sounds of air circulation, nor the routine actions of cleaning and maintenance crews. Nonetheless, there was some manner in which Cory perceived the landscape's lack of light without ever directly sighting Levin's surrounding smeared-ice plains, and some manner in which this knowledge informed his mood. During the daylit week, it was more straightforward to ignore the troublesome memories which resurfaced; the task of simply living, and getting by, and pushing indifferently towards contentment was a thing more readily achievable; he enjoyed those passages of time. There was work, and there was downtime, and it was enough. But the night pushed Cory, and fretted him, and forced him repeatedly to re-evaluate his current lack of longer-term direction. The night was a dangerous time, and Cory always knew when it fell.

Work was the only thing which helped, when the days were night. Work gave purpose and distraction from himself. When the work ran out… well, he would just have to find a way to ensure it didn't.

Snead's latest task was a simpler one, meshwork with no build component, just as Cory preferred; though it was nonetheless a strange one, and threw him deep into coding a purpose-built heat exchanger which Portia described for him, but which she refused to bring to the shop. Did the device actually exist? And if so, what possible purpose could it serve? The construction Snead sketched out bore no discernible connection to the task of flow measurement, nor to the other ostensible applications for which she had previously sought his services; and the rig seemed, from the sound of it, overengineered and needlessly complex. But when he questioned her on it, she refused to answer. That is, she would provide all the technical detail he would require, for she evidently did wish him to succeed in drawing up the coding she was paying him for, but its purpose did not concern him. It was an attitude he found exasperating. True, he did not need to understand the device's intended use to ensure that its outputs could be controlled in the necessary manner; but it would help with the task nonetheless. There was a sense in which her standoffishness, her occupational privacy (or whatever else he might want to call it) was insulting to him as a contractor. He was used to the habitual instinct towards uncommunicativeness of the small and somewhat homogeneous set of prospectors for whom he'd done occasional assignments; and that had been a level of secrecy for which the underlying motivation had been clear, to keep private a location they believed might hold the source of their wealth. With Portia, it went beyond this. In what possible way could the intended function of a heat exchanger compromise the secret of her location of interest? It couldn't, so far as Cory could see, and he came close to telling her so. Professionalism was not always a comfortable mantle.

The coding didn't take him too long, nor were there any problems that showed up in the testing, but he didn't deliver it to Snead straightaway. Instead, he made contact, said the task was causing him more difficulties than anticipated, an effect he hinted was contingent on her refusal to straightforwardly state the heat exchanger's purpose. Field equipment, she told him when he pressed; which was nonsense, because a heat exchanger wasn't something which had any purpose in the field, in isolation. The device was clearly intended to operate in tandem with at least one other item of equipment, to maintain a desired temperature; whether for habitation or safe mechanical operation or chemical processing made little difference from a fundamental engineering or coding perspective. She was right, he did not need to know. The task was sufficiently defined as it was.

And yet he wanted to know.

Still, it would not do to estrange a client. He completed the documentation, arranged the delivery. She paid promptly.

He was busy for ten weeks following this, a blessed, complicated, achievable assignment recoding, from scratch, the life-support overmind for a briefly derelict W&E arcology some two hours' travel time southwest of Levin. The work, conveniently, could all be handled from his own quarters. The client was one of his semi-regulars, a woman who ran a vehicle customisation shop in the light-industry precinct where he rented his own small workshop and office; now, it seemed, she was diversifying into housing. He couldn't see the commercial sense in her decision; the settlement had been abandoned as part of the slow general drift of manufacturing, commerce and population towards Sagan and the brilliant promise of the still-uncompleted elevator. Who would the refurbished arcology house? Who, in these difficult times, would choose to relocate to a community smaller and yet more isolated than Levin? But of course the work was welcome, and Cory began almost to feel secure and settled himself. Perhaps it might be a good future after all. He extended his lodgings for another twelvemonth, bought some new clothing and utensils.

Snead contacted him again five days before completion of the overmind refurbishment. The call was security-locked, and would not let him surro to an avatar. This time what she was after was clearly illegal: she was asking him for a vehicle spoofing-code package. He could supply it, but that wasn't the point; what she asked presented an unacceptable hazard to him. He refused. She called back. He took the call, explained in more detail the reasons why he would not perform the task (yet always concealing the true reason: that he did not dare be found out). She attempted to argue that the coding was not as problematic an assignment as he had stated. He interjected, disagreed. Then he cut the call, blocked contact from her.

She found a way to reach him, three hours later, using a messaging technique which had him wondering why she even required his services. *Can we meet? Please?* Nothing more.

His mind rife with unvoiced misgivings, he agreed.

Levin's pond was scarcely even that, just a carefully landscaped bleb of water, waist-deep at most, ten metres at its broadest, and fringed by a grassy embankment along which, so local legend had it, the settlement's public-spaces committee had once tried to establish a stand of willows. There were fish in the pond, and long strands of weed; it was widely stated that the pond also housed a few small turtles, though Cory had never seen them, and some species of freshwater crustacean. There were two benches for seating, on opposite sides, though placed with enough forethought that they weren't directly facing each other.

The pond wasn't one of Cory's favourite places in Levin; probably it wasn't one of anyone's favourite places. It tried too hard to be something it wasn't, which is always more difficult to sustain the longer the attempt is made. Cory knew a bit about that too.

Snead was late, and he remembered she'd done that last time as well. He wasn't sure whether she was simply one of those people to whom punctuality wasn't important, or whether there was something more calculated about the delay. After her subterfuge with the messaging trick, he was starting to suspect it was the latter.

He found himself thinking, then, of Arum, which he'd promised himself he would not do.

Snead arrived, with no pretence at hurrying. Nodded in greeting; did not say anything to him. Spent, instead, two minutes or so surveying the pond; and when she did turn her head to speak, it was not to say anything related to the contentious vehicle-spoofing codework.

'It's supposed to represent Ligeia in miniature,' Snead told him, gesturing vaguely towards the still water.

'Probably a good thing the willows didn't take, then,' Cory answered. Why did you ask to meet? he wondered.

She had turned again to stare into the pond's weed-strewn, sediment-hazed depths, as though she were searching out something lost, and her next statement was sufficiently sotto voce that he understood its content only in retrospect. 'It was wrong of me to ask that of you.'

He waited. Was she expecting apology?

'If you're still willing to undertake work, I have another task I can assign you. It's fairly complex, but it doesn't involve anything which should trouble you.' She reached up, brushed a strand of hair behind her ear. 'In any sense, I mean.'

He stayed silent for as long as he thought he could get away with. Noted to himself that, among many possible responses, observations and reactions percolating through his head, there was some sense of disappointment in himself at never having previously noted the similarity of the pond's shoreline to Ligeia. 'I'll need a bit more detail than that.'

'It's an integration project,' she replied. 'Propulsion control, attitude control, sensors, lifesystems, telemetry, failsafes. Some of the modules are your own, others are factory-supplied. They might be somewhat more challenging to integrate.'

'Propulsion control. It's a vehicle?'

'Yes.'

'What type?'

She moved a couple of paces along the pond's edge, turned briefly towards him in an invitation, he thought, to follow. He did so. She was staring into the water again when she responded. 'Custom.'

Fine, he thought. *Be secretive. It's your fucking superpower, isn't it?* 'I'd need an hourly rate. Thirty-five per, paid on a daily basis, in advance.' Which was a polite, or possibly not even polite, way of indicating that he didn't much care for the job. That wasn't entirely true, the work sounded as though it might be interesting, and if it adhered to the rudiments of her description then it was comfortably within his abilities. But her evasiveness, her churlish uninformativeness: she didn't trust him, plainly, and he struggled to see why he should trust her.

'I can't do that,' she replied. 'My reserves aren't limitless. But I can offer a fixed remuneration for the project which I think should recompense you fairly, of which I can offer thirty percent in advance.' She named a figure which, if anything, seemed excessive. If it was as she said, it would not require so many hours work.

'That's the remuneration?' he asked.

'That's thirty percent.'

He did not trust himself to answer straightaway, adopted her trick of attempting to scry the pond. 'I would have two requirements if I was to take this on,' he said. 'One is that I must have an absolute assurance that what you're doing, and what you're asking me to do, is not in any way against the law, here or elsewhere on Titan.'

'You have that assurance.'

'In writing?'

'That can be arranged. What's the other requirement?'

'I need to know what vehicle, what kind of vehicle, I'll be doing the coding for.'

'You'll see it, in due course. Obviously, the integration will need to be done in situ.'

'In situ?'

'There's some travel involved.'

Suited, and hefting a well-insulated coverall that was crammed half with clothing, half with tools and small instruments, he reported the next morning to the Levin East Vehicle Hangar.

She had an off-roader: a well-travelled Volker Duck 3, towing a high-pod trailer almost as large as itself. The slab-fronted Duck reinforced his hunch: it was one of a few standard vehicles preferred by prospectors, rugged, reliable; amphibious when necessary. The trailer, though, wasn't. He wondered at that, and at what the trailer's mass might be. The rig didn't look like a good combination for progressing further into the uplands, where tracks were few and gradients sometimes steep.

He did not remark on this; it wasn't his place. Nor did he respond to her clear dissatisfaction with the vehicle, visible in the body language evident even through her suit. She strode to the hire-office airlock, awaited entry; he stayed out in the hangar. Not his place.

Snead was ten minutes in the office; then she walked out, followed shortly after by an employee in a site supervisor's suit. Cory stood a little aside, still not knowing what was going on. He wondered whether the

Duck was the vehicle she wanted him to upgrade; somehow he doubted it. 'Propulsion' and 'attitude control' weren't terms one used on wheeled or tracked vehicles; they sounded more appropriate to an aerial craft. Or a boat.

A worker commandeered the Duck, drove it off towards a workspace at the hangar's far end. The engine noise on startup had reverberated unpleasantly, beyond the abilities of Cory's suit's adaptive acoustics to counter. Portia Snead still seemed to be involved in a conversation with the site supervisor; Cory hadn't been invited onto that channel.

The Duck rattled back several minutes later. Now the trailer was larger. There was a final exchange between Snead and the supervisor—concluded, Cory thought, with less than total amicability—and the supervisor returned to his airlocked office. Snead reinitiated comms with Cory.

'What was that about?' he asked, expecting one of her patent non-answers.

'The chisellers tried to short me on the trailer,' she replied. Her continued annoyance showed in her tone. 'I'd ordered a seven-metre, they had tried to palm me off with a five point five.'

'What's the trailer for?' he asked.

'You'll see.' And that, it seemed, was all he was going to get.

They finalised the credit transfer in the Duck's still-warming cab, breath clouding the bleach-sharpened air. He'd never been in a Duck before: it was more cramped than he had been expecting. A two-person cab, backed by rudimentary sleeping/living quarters and by a sealed closet he presumed to be an even more rudimentary toilet/shower stall. Headspace, it seemed, wasn't something the Duck's designers had rated highly. And the cab's accordion-style airlocks were barely big enough to remove and stow a suit, even at full extension.

Snead sparked the engine; the Duck's cab thrummed with latent, low-throated power. She ran through the lengthy safety pre-check with an efficiency that spoke of long familiarity: novice prospector she may be, but she evidently knew her way around the vehicle. Cory made an effort to memorise what he could of the vehicle's manual overrides.

She requested and received departure clearance from hangar control. The Duck lumbered forward, took a wide turn towards the vehicle exit hatch.

Suspension, it seemed, wasn't something the Duck's designers had rated highly, either.

'My name's not Snead,' she told him. They were headed north-east, or nearly so, along the well-established track that ran broadly parallel to the spine of the local range. It was early daylight, barely twelve hours after sun-up, the landscape sombre and indistinct in the still haze-dominated light. Slopes of umber, folds of deep shadow, pallid grainy sky. They had been travelling perhaps three hours, and had already passed a couple of poorly defined junctions that led into the mountains proper. Well, it stood to reason that any as-yet-unexploited site wouldn't have been so close to a sizeable settlement. Cory wondered how far they would be going. And about her unprompted confession, and its timing.

'What should I call you, then?' he asked, not bothering to hide a trace of sharpness in his tone.

'The Portia part is true.'

'You have a last name?'

'Mabaso.'

'What is it, exactly, that you do?'

He waited for elaboration, but she wasn't so inclined. It could have been that she was busy with the demands of driving; but Cory didn't believe it.

'How do you know my aunt?' he asked, still with the same voice.

The road, washboarded and potholed, bent around a large raised knuckle of sepia-stained ice. Cory grew resentful that she was ignoring his question; but, it transpired, she was deep in reverie, or memory.

'I worked with her,' she said at length, and there was awkwardness in her voice. 'Or rather, she worked with us. With Prof and me. Prof hired her for security.'

'Prof?'

'Wiremu Garrity,' she explained. 'My supervisor.'

'Supervisor?'

'Former supervisor.' There was something caught in the cords of her voice; Cory wasn't sure what.

'He's at wherever we're going?' Cory hazarded.

She steered the Duck onto a wide rutted berm, killed the drive function. Turned to face Cory, her eyes dark under a furrowed brow. 'He's a long way south of here. South-south-east, I suppose, if you want to be particular. He died, Cory. He was killed.' She took in a long breath, let it out, slow, seemed all the while to be staring straight through him. 'Ambushed.'

His cheeks flamed; he didn't respond. It was too redolent of what he'd sought to keep buried about his own past. He waited for her to proceed, because clearly there was more.

'And if the two of us hadn't swapped places half an hour before that, at Ter— at your aunt's suggestion, I'd have been killed instead. Or possibly in addition.'

'And my aunt?' Cory asked. 'How does she figure in this?'

'Cory,' she replied. The tone of those two syllables was ample. 'I am so sorry.'

two

They made good time on the first daycycle's drive, covering more than two hundred klicks in an eight-hour stint. The trackway leading northeast from Levin was not as well maintained as she would like, with potholes and subsidence and the occasional re-gouged streambed cutting across the trackway, but it was all within the Duck's capabilities. When she grew tired, after five hours or so, of overseeing the vehicle's operation, she allowed Cory to take the panel for a spell. His unfamiliarity with the vehicle's controls was evident, but scarcely problematic: the Duck was, for the most part, a fairly forgiving vehicle, able to find the path even when its operator could not. She could see him growing accustomed to the Duck's foibles, even in just an hour-long shift at the controls.

She kept the cab cold, the way she liked it. Cold driving was clear-headed driving, and if Cory disagreed with her thermal preference, he didn't say so. Indeed, he didn't say much of anything for the last few hours of driving for the day. She felt awkward about that. She'd had no right to keep from him for so long the fact and the circumstances of his aunt's death, and even now there was a substantial part she hadn't told him; but the time wasn't right. She didn't want, right now, to have to explore with him the difficult working relationship she had had with Teresa Maria: she had never trusted the woman. Or rather, while she'd never had cause to doubt the woman's loyalty, there had been something she couldn't trust about the unspoken burden which Teresa Maria had carried, plain in her eyes and in her carriage and in her demeanour. It was odd how it worked, though, because it had been exclusively on Teresa Maria's endorsement that Portia had decided to approach Cory, and she trusted Cory. For all that she had kept from him things she should not have kept from him. There would have to be a way found to rectify that. Later.

They had stopped, that first spell of driving, just ten klicks short of Czaplinski; and if he wondered at this decision, wondered why Portia did not push on into the small settlement itself for less unreasonably confined lodgings than those provided within the Duck, then again he did not voice this. Probably Cory thought her miserly, refusing the small expense of comfortable accommodation. In truth it was simply that she preferred the isolation of a stop in the wilderness, conveniently close to the settlement if an emergency arose, but sufficiently far to avoid attracting the attention which fell to everyone passing through such a small community, with inhabitants wishing to know one's purpose, one's destination, one's goal. Given she had not yet divulged this information to Cory, she was even less inclined to reveal it to a stranger, or a group of strangers.

It was difficult to trust people. It hadn't always been so.

Such was the bitter fruit of the ambush. She'd lost a mentor, colleague, and close friend; she'd lost someone else who might, in time, have become something of a friend; and she'd lost a large part of herself, as she'd been before. It had taken her months to learn how to be with that; she was still learning. Still awoke, on occasion, besieged, confused, threatened by absent danger.

She started suiting up, explained she was going outside for a spell. Told him he could accompany her, or not, as he wished. In truth, she hoped he'd stay in the Duck. There wasn't any purpose to her excursion beyond a need for space: the cab was cramped, and she was not accustomed, these days, to spending protracted intervals in such proximity with anyone who was not Prof.

True, her suit was also cramped, but she had expended so much time in fieldwork in recent years that the suit was simply a thicker skin.

26

The airlock cycled; she climbed out.

The sun was now high enough, the haze and cloud thick enough that half the marbled sky glowed beige with slow-shifting rivulets of comparative brightness, as photons sought their best way through the obstructive layers. Towards the east and south, beyond the Duck's angular, greeny-blue superstructure—its headlights and running lights still aglow—a weathered line of hills, time-worn almost to nubs of stained ice; a ridgeline beyond that, taller, darker, stretched like a child's sketch, smudged by distance, brown crayon on parchment. The sporadically visible peaks of yet further hills. None of them, not even the highest, was worthy of the description 'mountain'; they perhaps had been, once, but erosion by windblown haze flakes and methane rain had diminished them.

It was a landscape that gave nothing, promised nothing, and the Duck—its as-yet-empty rented trailer fastened behind it like the ideation of some afterthought—looked supremely out of place. There was no good reason to stop here, other than her dislike of mingling with strangers.

She turned her back on the Duck. Walked a short distance, alone with the sounds of her T-suit's processes, until she reached the streambed they would need to cross tomorrow morning: gravelled ice, tholin drifts softening some of the contours. It wouldn't present any problems.

Those would come later.

Was this the right thing she was doing? Probably not; it was a fool's errand. There was minimal chance of success, and the risk of catastrophe was significant. Those traces might have been anything, as Prof himself had always conceded; and she had never been as convinced, never felt the need to be as convinced, as he had seemed. There'd be nothing to find. If the landscape promised anything, it promised that. But she must try, nevertheless.

She stayed out another fifteen minutes or so, thinking thoughts she had no way of conveying to anyone other than Prof; then she returned to the Duck, and climbed back into the airlock.

*

From the moment she removed her helmet, caught as off-guard as ever by the singed whiff of tholins, her passenger was full of questions. She should probably have expected that, should probably have prepared for it; she hadn't. She wasn't ready for this.

'How did my aunt die?' There was an edge of brittle accusation. Understandable, and somewhat effective. Portia struggled with feelings of guilt, had done ever since, though there had been nothing she could have done which could have saved Cory's aunt. Nothing, other than to have not allowed Teresa Maria to take her place in the freight hauler's cab, in a situation where there had been no forewarning of danger.

Portia stuck to the mechanics of the process. She'd explain motives later. Told him about the ambush on the Via Australis, with more detail this time. How Wiremu Garrity and Teresa Maria, in the Longhauler's cab, had stood no chance, a shot to the windscreen bestowing a messy death by asphyxiation. The vehicle had skidded off the raised trackway, had toppled sideways. Portia had been in the passenger quarters behind the cab. Jolted alert, she'd tried the hatch through to the cab— inoperable—and had then suited quickly. She'd crawled through the airlock into the freight housing, thinking that its rear hatch promised an exit from the vehicle where the airlocks were now both inaccessible. She'd been mistaken, though: the goods in the freight housing were strewn everywhere, and the aisle to the rear hatch was blocked by toppled crates, spilled produce, and dented and ruptured containers.

What had caused the crash? Her mind had conjured possibilities: a faulty drive cluster causing the vehicle to slew; fatigue; or perhaps a volatiles pocket buried beneath the road's ice surface, breached by the Longhauler's weight. There was, surely, some innocent explanation, though the damage was likely severe. It would set them back considerably, possibly by months. She tried contacting Prof, then Teresa Maria, gained no response, and at this she grew more sharply worried, because the likelihood was that one or both of them was hurt. It came to her, then, that among the sounds around the vehicle there was weapons fire.

The next several minutes had been tortuous. By the time she'd emerged from the passenger quarters, the life had ebbed from Prof and Cory's aunt, and the three assailants also lay dead or dying.

There were parts she didn't understand at all. Those pharmhands hadn't all killed themselves, but there was nobody else. It horrified her, refused any easy explanation for the deaths, whether for Prof and Teresa Maria or for the ambushers.

'And you… fled?' Cory asked, still sharp-voiced. 'You didn't wait for the pol?'

'Cory, it was Ontario Lacus; there was no pol to speak of, not within several hours. And I didn't want to wait around for reinforcements.'

Cory was silent, then, for some seconds. 'What were you carrying?'

'Cargo, mostly,' she told him. That wasn't a lie. 'There was something we had to test in the field; we'd bid for the haulage from the food factories at Yelle, carting it to the settlements north and west of there. Prof had hoped that that would give us cover; obviously, it didn't. I don't think any of us really apprehended the risk.' Not even your aunt. But she couldn't add that. On top of everything else, it would sound like accusation.

'What were you testing? In the field?'

'A… scientific instrument.'

'That doesn't really tell me anything,' Cory complained.

'I know that,' she replied, after a pause. 'There are parts of this I need to tell you, but I can't. Not yet.'

'What kind of bullshit answer is that?'

'It's difficult.'

'You don't trust me.'

'That is most definitely not the case. If I mistrusted you, would I have walked out of the Duck just now, left you to get up to whatever you wanted for thirty minutes or so, in here? Or to just leave?'

'What, so that was a trust exercise?'

'No, I needed space. But the query's still valid. There are aspects of this that need groundwork, because they will just sound implausible otherwise.'

29

'So give me the groundwork,' said Cory.

'Tomorrow,' said Portia. 'Right now I need something to eat.' She stood up, moved to the rack of ready-prepareds. Passed him one, without first asking what he wanted or even if he was hungry.

They ate without complicating matters with further conversation, almost as though they had agreed, at least, on this.

They finished the meals. 'Thank you,' he said, as she dropped the spent casings into the cycler.

Then there was a conversation, not quite strained but decidedly stilted, as though they were rival predators who did not quite have the measure of each other. A safer topic of discussion: origins, rather than endings. Portia already knew several of the details of Cory's childhood, through her dealings with Teresa Maria, though she was careful to act as though all the information regarding Cory's upbringing in Ponnamperuna was genuinely new to her. Much of it was, of course, or at least viewed from a different vantage, the self rather than the family history. For her own part, it was difficult to restrict herself to the years before her work with Prof: she did not often revisit, nowadays, her childhood in Hunten, her schooling, her family life. She found herself commenting, without knowing whether it was genuinely her own view or merely something which she had assimilated, on the different sense of society that existed in large versus small settlements. It was, for her part, somewhat calculated: she needed to regain Cory's trust, to return to the position of equilibrium—of opposing but balanced tensions—which had operated between them before her incomplete disclosure regarding Teresa Maria's death, regarding the events preceding it, and regarding the goal of her current trek northward from Levin.

Tomorrow, she'd said. She would tell him, tomorrow, the things he wished to know. He would want to know more than he needed, she was certain of that; but what she was not certain about was how she could broach it. As tomorrow grew closer, the difficulties intensified.

He didn't protest when she called an end to the awkward dialogue, when she rose to prepare for sleep. She took her toiletries and her sleepwear into the hygiene cubicle, latched the door, allowed her facial muscles to briefly relax for the first time in hours. Shoulders likewise.

When she emerged, he was already settled on one of the Duck's two sleeping berths, and on the edge of sleep. She took the other berth and tried with only partial success to ignore his snoring, which started soon after.

She woke without quite believing that sleep had occurred, established— the Duck; its air; its odours; the background sounds of the vehicle's heating and air-purifying mechanisms; the more foregrounded sounds of Cory's snoring, more subdued and yet somehow more grating than Prof's had been; her own already wide-strewn thoughts—that sleep could not be re-attained for now, decided she should rise. She moved, cold-footed and in a barely semi-conscious stumble, through to the front bench, did a brief systems check, and then initiated the drive sequence. The power was available instantly, but the mech would need several minutes to warm to a safe operating temp. While she waited, she imbibed two slugs of coffee, the first one cold. By the time the board glowed green everywhere that truly mattered, she was fully alert. The Duck moved forward, its motion slow and uncertain for the first hundred metres as she steered it back over the uneven ground to the trackway. It blundered through the streambed, drew within sight of Czaplinski—a three-storey blockish structure, population double digits—before Cory woke. She didn't interrupt his morning routine; was in fact rueing the impending loss of solitude.

They bypassed Czaplinski. At the junction north she turned left; the trackway rounded an ancient ridge, then headed due north with a precision that would have gratified any cartographer. Cory had by this point come forward into the cab. It was clear he harboured questions, but none emerged for the next ten klicks or so.

'Where are we heading?' he asked, at last.

'Hörst,' she replied. 'Two-hundred-odd yet, it'll probably take us another eight hours at this rate.'

'It's our destination?'

'We'll be stopping there,' she said. 'Briefly. But no, it's not our destination.'

'Where is our destination, then?' he asked.

'The trackway ends at Cottini.'

'So what's at Cottini?'

'Not much, in all honesty. But you'll see for yourself.'

He stood in silence behind the bench for a while more: it irritated her, but not enough to rebuke him over it. She knew, for her part, that her own reticence to divulge must irk him. Then he went to attend to something in the vehicle's living quarters, she didn't know what. When, later, he returned and sat beside her, he asked if she would like a break from the driving. The task didn't bother her, the way presented no difficulties for the Duck, but she acquiesced. Took herself back to the sleeping berth, for nothing more than a momentary rest. Awoke an indeterminate spell of time later, her mouth jaded and fuzzed, her hip sore. The Duck was running faster, thrumming at a pitch she didn't entirely approve of. She slid out of the berth, went through to the cab. The cab was warmer than she approved, too.

'Skid-bike,' Cory said, gesturing at the rear scope. 'Been following us from Czaplinski, according to the log.' He bent over the panel, increased gain on the image, magnified it further.

She didn't see what the effort had added. Not any useful detail, anyway. The twin lamps characteristic of an older-model skid-bike, a dark and uncertain upright shape which shook more from the Duck's cam's processing deficiencies than from the bike's motion. A poorly resolved focal point in a bland landscape of tholin-rusted and rubbled ice beneath a grey-brown sky. She slid in beside Cory, fiddled the cam's settings herself, strove to minimise the shake, to enhance the contrast; gave up. Toyed with the thought of engaging Cory to reprogram the cam: it was, she knew, within his capabilities. But it would pose a distraction, and she didn't need distractions.

The skid-bike must be a kilometre or more behind them. But it was noticeable enough, and this she found somewhat reassuring. 'Probably they've got business at Hörst,' she replied.

'Maybe,' he said. 'Feels strange, though.'

'Why so?'

'They've stayed behind us since Czaplinski.'

'That doesn't make it strange. There's only one way to get from Czaplinski to Hörst.'

'Yes, but.' He made a noise she couldn't quite define. 'They could easily have passed us several times. But they haven't.'

'Novice rider?' she suggested. 'Someone unsure of the bike's handling, taking it slow?'

'I don't think you believe that any more than I do,' he said. 'The trackway's well enough maintained, and linear to the point of boredom.'

She didn't respond directly. Instead she checked the chrono, checked the map. 'I can take over from here,' she hinted.

They reached Hörst. There was some problem with the short-stay booking at the vehicle hangar, the nature of which the superintendent couldn't adequately explain. Certainly it wasn't lack of space: the short-stay lot, nestled out in the open between the hangar itself and the skyport, was less than forty percent occupied, and this seemed unlikely to change for the few hours they'd need here. In the end, as was often the case in smaller settlements such as this, additional credit resolved the impasse; but the interaction left her with a lingering mood of annoyance. She parked, suited up, walked the short distance to the hangar airlock, entered the settlement proper.

She'd advised Cory to stay with the Duck.

'Is this about the skid-bike?' he'd asked.

'Not at all,' she'd said. The bike had fallen back, or had stopped, sometime around two hours after Cory had first brought it to her attention. It bothered her more that it had stopped, truth be told, than that it might have followed them the whole way to Hörst. What was there out here to stop *for*, between settlements? 'I'd just rather not have to wonder about where you might've got to when it's time to leave.'

'I'll miss my one opportunity to explore Hörst,' he'd said, in mock-complaint.

'There's nothing much to miss,' she'd replied.

'What are we stopping for here again anyway?'

'Oxygen,' she'd replied. It was a half-truth, but close enough. 'And some more ready-prepareds.'

'There's enough for another week already. Isn't that enough?'

'I always like to have choice,' she'd said. That, too, was a half-truth.

She stowed her suit in a locker just off the settlement's western concourse, walked what seemed to her an unnecessary distance to the nearest sales point. Hörst was spacious, almost empty, its interior both well-maintained, unworn, and badly dated, as though it had been designed for a much larger population than had ever arrived. Brightly coloured polymer tiles underfoot, lengthy murals interspersed with large-scale viewscreens which panned slowly through feeds of the dunefields, the hills, the smaller lakes: it was clean, it was warm, it was all not entirely believable.

Perhaps she shouldn't have insisted that Cory stay with the Duck. He'd been agreeable enough at the suggestion, though. Possibly he saw it as an opportunity to try to learn, from the Duck's systems, what her purpose was out here near the limits of Titan's habitation. Well, he was welcome to the effort, but she doubted he'd have much success.

At the sales point she arranged for delivery, within the next ninety minutes, of enough ready-prepareds to last the pair of them another two weeks, or one of them a month. More would've attracted curiosity, which was best avoided. She added four hectolitres of water, culinary grade, to the order. Then she checked in with the gas supplier.

'Portia Snead,' she announced, when the supplier's avatar coalesced. 'I have an order for helium, ten cubic metres, six nines.'

Happily, they had the shipment.

There was one further call. She could as easily have placed it in the cab of the Duck rather than here, but for Cory.

At least, that was her excuse. But she wondered whether she might not be losing her enthusiasm for the project. What was she hoping to achieve, and who was she looking to impress? Prof was beyond noticing, now, anything she would supposedly be doing in his name or in his honour.

Did it matter to *her*? And was that enough? She stood at the sales point for two minutes, three, trying to decide. Then she placed the call, which was characteristically brief and to-the-point, and headed back to the short-stay lot to await the deliveries.

'What's in the trailer?' he asked, as soon as she'd climbed back aboard the Duck.

She turned the heating down before she responded. 'Hello to you too.' There was something furtive about him, she thought, and her suspicion firmed that he'd tried to uncover the Duck's secrets while she'd been in Hörst. He was standing in the very centre of the living quarters, fists bunched, scowling.

'I'm getting tired of the evasion, the delays, the false pretences. You'll tell me the exact nature of this assignment you've hired me for, or I'll make my own way back.'

He was angrier than she'd seen him yet. In all likelihood, he'd checked out the trailer for himself in her absence, had seen that it carried nothing of significance. Nothing for him to work on. She'd have to handle this carefully, with at least enough honesty to mollify him.

'Currently, there's just supplies in the trailer. Maybe you knew that already.'

'What are you suggesting? And why the fuss over the trailer size, back in Levin, if all it's for is a couple cubic metres of storage?'

'We'll need it tomorrow.'

'Tomorrow? It's always bloody tomorrow with you. The flow of intel is strictly one way. I've been patient, but I'm done. You'll tell me now. I won't be a party to anything illegal.'

'I know,' she replied. Paused, met his eye. Held it while she added, 'I've never been a party to anything illegal.'

'The hell do you mean by that?'

'I know why it's important for you to keep your nose clean from now on. We both know that.'

'Are you blackmailing me?'

'No, Cory, I'm not. I just wouldn't.'

'But nothing illegal? That's a lie. You wanted to hire me to spoof the vehicle signature. For starters.'

'That was a mistake. I should not have asked that of you. But I thought you could—'

'You thought I could what?'

She was silent for too long, felt herself choked by a sense of dread. She dare not lose Cory's assistance. Not because his abilities were in any way irreplaceable, but because she didn't see how to take matters past this. She had followed Prof too far, had moved past Prof when he'd fallen. She needed to see this through; but the doubts were breeding. 'Look,' she said at last, 'if the lack of operational details at this point is too big an obstacle to you—and I understand, you're a practical person, you need detail to function reliably, I'm like that myself, believe it or not—if it's too much, or not enough, that's fine. I will not betray any confidences of yours. You have my word on that, though I appreciate that may not count overmuch with you. I can tell you that what I'm seeking to do, what I'm looking for your help with, your expertise, is not in any way against the law, is severely unlikely to be in any way lucrative, may very well not pan out. You'll get paid for your work regardless. But having seen Prof Garrity ambushed and killed, having seen your aunt killed, over what we are currently trying to test out, I dare not risk anything that would draw attention to what it is we're heading towards. That is, what we're possibly heading towards.'

'You're implying that telling me what this is about would draw attention to this mysterious destination of yours. That's ridiculous.'

'Is it?'

'Of course it is.'

'Cory, I have no way of knowing how you will react. What you might inadvertently let slip. As long as this looks like two novice prospectors out on a long-shot foray—'

'You're telling me it's not?'

'No. That's the cover story. I will brief you soon, properly, you have my word on that, but we need to collect the vehicle first.'

'Vehicle? The one the modwork is for?'

She nodded. 'Tomorrow. Just shy of Cottini. Speaking of which, we'd better motor. Are you in?'

Cory stared at her, looked around at the shelf of ready-prepareds, turned to glance into the cab. Turned back to Portia. 'Fuck it,' he said.

Past Hörst, the terrain and the trackway both grew rougher, and the going was consequently slower. Nothing the Duck couldn't handle—ruts, washboarding, potholes; typical inundation damage—but the limitations of its suspension were made more apparent to its occupants as they put the additional kilometres behind them. An hour into the spell, the road started to climb into the dirty beige hills which had been flanking them since leaving Hörst. The grade was shallow, but the occasional tight turn was a challenge with the trailer, and as they rose towards the pass Portia grew uneasy at the steep slope down to the left. She had travelled this road once before, she thought, several years ago, with Prof: her recollection was that the route had then had safety barriers, and a lip to channel runoff. Both were gone now. Perhaps it had been a different trackway? But the hillsides looked familiar nonetheless, as though some long-submerged eidetic memory was surfacing in her mind.

There was a particularly solid jolt, as the Duck hit some defect or dip. Portia bit her cheek and swore, running back through the windscreen's log to see if she could spy whatever they'd hit. Whatever it had been, it didn't show. She batted away Cory's offer to take over the steering. As if that would make any difference—under these conditions it was largely the Duck's risk-averse algorithms which were in control of their fate. Aside from that bump, it had been performing well.

'What happens if we meet another vehicle?' Cory asked.

'We won't,' Portia replied, trying to sound confident. She sharpened the cab's chill to help her focus.

The top of the saddle brought a vista of peaks and gullies, shaded in variegated sepia. There was the suggestion of a haze-shrouded plain further ahead, rimmed to the right by a long ridge that was most probably an eroded crater wall. But their way would swing well clear of that: northwest across the plain, towards Cottini.

The eastern half of the sky was distinctly darker than the western: this far north, this time of Saturn's year, the daylight didn't last more than three-and-a-half days. The rest of the fortnight was night-time.

She checked the chrono, weighed their schedule. 'Can you rest for a spell?' she asked Cory. 'I'll get us down out of the hills, but I'll need a break after that. And we should push on to Cottini without a stopover if we can.'

'Yeah, I can take over in a couple hours' time,' said Cory, getting up from the bench. 'But why the rush? Do we have an appointment?'

'Not exactly. But let's just say the timing's tight.'

Once he'd gone back through to his berth in the living quarters, she dialled the cab's temperature down another notch, and focussed on the road ahead. It was steeper down, in parts, than it had been on the ascent, and she felt as though she had to take more notice of what the trailer might do on the steepest sections.

There was a further five hours of driving once they were out of the foothills. Cory took the brunt of that, while Portia tried to rest up. But it wasn't working, so she resorted to medicated sleep, and consequently awoke with more difficulty when her berth roused her. Her head hurt; she was nagged by a dream she already couldn't remember. She drank a half-litre of water so cold it made her teeth hurt, wolfed down a protein snack, moved forward into the cab, took her seat. Why did he insist on turning it up so hot?

Out here on the plain, there were no landmarks to speak of, just the trackway and a smudge on the horizon that might, or might not, be Cottini. A greater proportion of the sky was darker now: it would be twilight, at best, when they reached Cottini, and fully dark tomorrow when they arrived at the proving ground. She wondered, now, whether that part of the schedule could have been better organised: it wasn't going to be easy to troubleshoot the vehicle's performance through the long darkness. But there hadn't been any other windows which could be arranged; it was always going to be this way. They'd manage, or they wouldn't.

The panel told her there were another sixty-five kilometres to Cottini, forty to the junction. At this rate, Cory would have them at the turnoff in just over an hour. It was treatment the Duck wasn't accustomed to. But she didn't berate him over it, simply hinted that she could take over at the controls again. At the third such hint, he moved aside for her.

'What is it at Cottini?' he asked.

'It's not Cottini itself. The place we're heading is an hour or so before it.'

'Which is what?'

'You'll see.'

The track that led in to the old foodworks was rougher than any they'd travelled on yet; but it was short, and the terrain was flat. On the road in, she explained to Cory that the foodworks had been derelict for the best part of a decade. It had been an ill-advised niche produce venture in a region where the population hadn't increased in line with demographic projections; indeed, it had, if anything, decreased over the past decade, with those remaining in the region not necessarily concerned with the purchase of expensive 'genuine fruit and vegetables' when the synthetic alternatives were cheap, nutritionally balanced and convenient.

'There's just the one inhabitant now,' she said.

'Which is who?'

'You'll see.'

But when they reached the parking apron at the rear of the complex, she was surprised to see that there were two vehicles already parked there.

One was an older-style skid-bike, its twin headlights gleaming briefly in reflection of the Duck's own as Portia steered the six-wheeler in close to what she hoped was the airlock.

three

Once he and Portia had passed through the decommissioned foodworks' airlock, they stowed their suits in lockers that might have been cloned from those found in the arrivals or departures halls of any transport hub. The air was cold and not of great quality, but Cory knew that sometimes it just took a minute to get accustomed to it. His suit would've warned him if it was worse than that.

They exited the locker room—Portia seemed to know where they were going—and were met, in a dirty tangerine corridor, by a man and a woman. The man was tall, dark-skinned, slender, his hair clipped so short it wasn't possible to be sure whether it was blond, grey, or white; Cory suspected the latter, in keeping with the rheumy eyes and wrinkled brow. No stoop, though, in his posture. The woman was younger, maybe Portia's age, closer to Cory's own height, of stocky build and with a shock of blue bioluminescent hair atop a face marked by uncorrected cryoscarring, lending the unfortunate appearance of a permanent, or at least frequent, scowl. Both wore dark clothing that might have been a uniform, might merely have been convergent fashion choices. Neither looked especially friendly.

It was obvious from Portia's reactions that she had expected the man. It was also apparent that she neither expected nor recognised the woman. But there wasn't really an opportunity for Cory to take joy in the fact that Portia no longer commanded the situation. If things were now not proceeding to the schedule she had carefully concealed from him, he nonetheless didn't see how that could be anything but an adverse circumstance for him. If anything, it meant even less opportunity for him to exert any influence on events, though more to ponder what his role was in this.

It was the woman who spoke first. 'Portia. Cory. We've been expecting you.'

The free use of her name seemed to further discommode Portia. 'What is this?' she asked, louder than necessary.

'That's what I'm hoping you can answer,' said the woman. 'But we needn't stand here on ceremony—Mr Xu has a nicely serviceable office which I believe can seat everyone.'

The accent wasn't a local's, but it wasn't like Portia's either: more clipped, more 'correct', but with the underlying hint of a lisp. It wasn't a Sagan accent, Cory decided, but it could well be the accent of someone with aspirations to live in Sagan.

If so, out here in the wilds of northern Farside, those vocal cords were a long way from where they wished to be.

'What is this?' Portia asked again. She sounded suddenly tired, or maybe defeated.

Xu's office wasn't in the same building, but there were walkways which, though brutally cold and sufficiently ammoniacal to sting the eyes, at least saved them the necessity of suiting up once more. Cory, at the rear, tried to get a sense of the spaces they were led through by the fast-walking Xu: industrial grey corridors mounted with darkened displays which, had they been alive, might have provided needed colour; storerooms with ranks of freestanding shelves, many of them bare; sizeable halls full of disused apparatuses which Cory expected were hydroponic rigs or something similar; a cafeteria space which gleamed but smelled too dismal to inspire confidence, as though perishables had travelled there, months ago, to die; other halls empty of anything more than a couple of pieces of office furniture and, in one instance, a bedframe; a second, smaller cafeteria which was evidently in current or recent use; some doors closed and completely unmarked. In some stretches—those closest to the life-support mechanisms, he suspected—there were small zones of comparative warmth. Elsewhere, there were the sounds of machinery, too distance-distorted to properly parse. It was a large complex, and Cory struggled to believe that there had ever been a reliably perceived need for this level of industry in such a sparsely settled region.

The lighting was the only constant: ceiling panels, ubiquitous, glowing cold white. It might as easily have been an abandoned hospital, brought back to some semblance of active operation, as a derelict foodworks. Or even a school.

Xu's office was gratifyingly warm. Xu himself sat behind the desk, Portia and Cory were offered seats opposite. There was a seat, too, for the stocky blue-haired woman, though she remained standing. On the wall behind her was a static image, flat, almost monochrome, of three people. Elsewhere on the walls, especially behind Xu and his desk, there were shelves, on which were stacked books, discs, and randomly arrayed small objects which Cory supposed might serve as souvenirs or mementoes: two air-tank adaptors, a damaged glove-sleeve flange, several emergency trigs. The most populous objects on the shelves, however, were figurines, most between ten and twenty centimetres in height. They appeared to be made of wood. A display of wealth?

'It's taken quite a while to find you,' said the woman, interrupting Cory's inspection of the room. 'But all I'm after, really, is information.'

'Are you?' asked Portia. 'Then you can start by giving us some of your own. A name would be good, at least.'

'Kalpana,' said the woman. She rubbed her wrist as though distracted, shuffled slightly sideways so she was now eclipsing more of the static image Cory had seen on the wall. 'Kalpana Braun. Soderblom pol.'

Cory didn't have good control over his blush reflex; he was careful not to react outwardly to that precarious last word. Where even was Soderblom, anyway? He wasn't sure, but nowhere near. Not round Levin, not round Ponnamperuna. Not within a thousand kilometres of anywhere he'd been. That was a point in his favour. If she'd been Ponnamperuna pol, or Neimann, or somewhere else in that vicinity, he would have had major difficulty checking his distress. In any case, the woman appeared more focussed on Portia for the moment; probably it was her she was here for, whatever that purpose might be. But there was still the blush, and that would cause him to draw attention to himself sooner or later. Plus she'd known his name.

How had she known his name? It wasn't even on his suit, so Braun couldn't have learnt it through simple telemetry.

With his presence here, would she figure him an accomplice? And to what?

'You would seem,' Portia commented, 'to be a bit out of area.' Which made it sound as though she, at least, knew where Soderblom was. But her voice betrayed moderate nervousness.

'That I am,' said Braun, her accent seeming to slip with those words. 'But this isn't the first time our paths have crossed, I think, though neither of us knew it at the time.'

'Please don't speak in riddles,' said Portia.

It was all Cory could do to not snort at that.

'Ontario Lacus,' said Braun, and Cory's face dropped ten Kelvin.

Portia twitched. 'You—that was *pol?*' she asked, rising from her chair, the question's sharply rising note seeming to detonate in Cory's ears. She was trembling with barely throttled rage. 'That was unprovoked, that was murder, that was—'

'It was all of those things,' said Braun, holding her hands palm-upward, speaking loud. 'But it wasn't pol, and if I'd had any idea such an attack was planned, I'd have acted to stop it sooner. I'm deeply sorry I did not. You have my condolences.' She seemed to catch sight of Cory for the first time, gazed directly at him, reiterated, 'You both have my condolences. Though I know how little that counts for. As does the fact that those responsible were themselves killed.'

'And now you ambush us here,' snapped Portia.

Cory found his voice. 'Wait,' he said to Braun. 'What in hell was your role in that? In my aunt's death?'

Braun turned her gaze towards him. The muscles in her cheek twitched, pulling her cryo-scar briefly upward. 'Soderblom was looking to build a case against the blues, against Tulleyrand,' she said, speaking more softly now. 'I was undercover for them. I'd been initiated into the group for a few months, was kept out of the loop on the planning for the heist, but was sent along as muscle.'

'Muscle?' Portia asked, a touch of deprecation in her voice as she met the eyes of the other woman.

'Muscle,' said Braun, with enough definition to the word to suggest the attribute was not for debate. 'It was supposed to be ambush, robbery at weapons-point, nothing more. That was how it was briefed to me. But Halinka—Stieg Tulleyrand's mistress—evidently had other plans, and the reactions of the other two indicated they were in on it as well. Either Tulleyrand was too, or Halinka was looking to cause trouble for him; they'd been rocky of late. None of that really matters. When she primed the PMP, I knew I needed to act fast. But I hadn't been entrusted with a weapon for myself. And I wasn't fast enough to grab one before it went to shit.'

'You were *there*?' Cory asked. 'When my aunt, and Portia's friend—'

'My supervisor,' said Portia.

'When they were killed?'

'Yes,' said Braun, still addressing Cory. 'As was Portia, of course, but I did not know that then. If I'd known, I would have taken her with me on the skid-bike, to Soderblom, so the pol could start piecing together what had happened, and to ensure her safety. There was no point in trying to do anything for anyone else by that stage. But I didn't linger; I fled the scene. I wasn't sure whose reinforcements would arrive first.'

'How does that work?' Cory asked. 'They were armed, quite heavily from the sound of it, and you weren't, and yet it's you who walked away alive.'

'I moved across to Jurgensen, punched through his airtank, took his gun. Then I shot the other two. Halinka was still trying to reload the PMP, and Jun-Ichi was climbing to access the vehicle's freight hatch.'

'Nobody punches through an airtank,' said Portia.

'Bone, no, but you'd be surprised what C-fibre prosthetics are capable of.'

'And how do you happen to have C-fibre prosthetics?'

'Long story. Another time, perhaps.'

'Is any of this true?' Portia asked. 'I mean, we have only your word on any of this.'

'It's true,' said Braun, pausing as another tic tugged briefly at her cryo-scar. 'There is helmcam vid of the attack, but I surrendered that to Soderblom. Other than that, no, there's no confirmation. But you yourself must've seen the aftermath. I'd suggest that if you want me to believe you, you need to start by believing me.'

'I don't give a tholin whether you believe me or not, so I've no need—'

'Believe it or not,' Braun interrupted, 'I'm relieved to see you alive.'

Portia stared at her, allowed several seconds to ebb away to the air-circ's quiet and slightly erratic seething. 'Just what the fuck is it you want with us? Or specifically, with me?' She gulped, dragged her face down and then up on a circular path, keeping eye contact the while. 'Is this an official investigation by the Soderblom pol? I find it very difficult to believe they would send just one officer on a long-haul trip across a hemisphere like this. Particularly an undercover officer who, it would have to be said, and based on your own words, after all, would have to be seen as compromised in various ways.' She did something with her mouth, as though she was playing with her lip. 'So what actually *is* this?'

'I told you,' said Kalpana Braun. 'I only want information. An understanding of what you were doing at Ontario. What you're looking for now. Thousands of klicks away.'

'Good luck with that,' said Cory, feeling the return of the blush's bloom as the words escaped him. All three turned to look at him, even Xu who had been sitting mute in his own office chair throughout this, running his hand over one of the possibly wooden figurines on his desk. Cory wasn't at all sure what their nominal host was making of all this.

'To answer your question,' said Braun, turning to face Portia once more, 'no, this is not an official pol action. I'm on indefinite leave

46

pending consideration of my actions. But I need to know for myself what it was I was a part of, and I need to know why it happened. I know the pharmhand side, but I don't know the rest. You, Portia, are very possibly the only person who can tell me that now.'

'I could, but I won't,' said Portia. 'Because either you wouldn't believe me, or you would believe me. One of those is pointless and the other is probably what got Wiremu Garrity and Cory's aunt killed.'

'I may be able to answer some of your questions also,' Braun replied mildly.

'There's nothing I want to ask you. We're here for one purpose only, and right now you are just in the way of that.'

'I can give you an assurance—'

'You know what?' Portia asked. 'Fine. You want words? Here they are. Off the record, if that counts for anything at all with you. We are here, Cory and I are here, to access a submersible constructed by Jethro Xu's family's engineering firm as a prototype. That submersible will be used to attempt to discover and retrieve from Ligeia Mare the wreckage of the discarded re-entry heat shield from the third uncrewed discovery mission to Titan, way back in 2040. Ontario Lacus was to have been a proving dive—'

'You weren't to know Tulleyrand's pharmhands had a base on the lake,' said Braun.

'On the lake?'

'Refurbed bulk cargo pod. Pontooned, tricked out in thermal camo, damn near invisible even from up close. It wasn't their only base, but it was an important one.'

'Was?'

'The intel from my undercover stint did *some* good,' said Braun. 'Proving dive, you said.'

Whatever words followed for the next minute or two, Cory didn't follow them. Because Kalpana Braun had moved slightly to the right, enough that the faux-monochrome image on the wall was no longer obscured.

The image contained someone he recognised.

*

47

When the talking was over, when Braun was satisfied with the details of Portia's explanations of intent and shortly before they were escorted to the room where Cory and Portia would sleep, he found a way to approach Jethro Xu and to ask, with a very bad approximation of merely casual interest, how long ago the image on his wall had been recorded.

Five years, Xu said. Which, all in, provoked more questions than it answered.

Night had fallen when Cory next arose, in the unfamiliar and temporarily disorienting confines of the cramped storeroom in which floorspace had last night been scavenged for two cots. Dust flakes drifted in the air, drawn languidly across the room by the ventilating system; his breath steamed; the heating seemed to have failed at some point in the past hours. An illumination panel was flickering.

He sat up carefully, guided his feet into the thermalwear moccasins he'd placed in easy reach.

Portia, it seemed, was already up. Cory wasn't sure he'd slept; it had been difficult to feel settled in the unfamiliar space of the foodworks. He couldn't understand the structure's purpose, couldn't see the motivation for Xu's habitation here. The man was evidently sufficiently wealthy to bear the not-inconsiderable costs in restoring an abandoned facility of this size to habitability, and the substantial costs in maintaining it; but there seemed to be no ambition to do more than that, to render it active once again, to monetise it in some fashion or other. It appeared merely to have become a place to live, in a location that offered little and with an infrastructure which demanded much. It was a large complex; oversized, given this region's small and hardly growing population: Cory didn't think they'd been led through all of the structure, but conversely didn't feel as though any areas had been proscribed from casual inspection as he and Portia had been shepherded from the airlock to Xu's office, from the office to the dorm room. Jethro Xu had talked, last night, of his plans to reinstate the foodworks, to adapt it as a grow site for luxury botanicals: spices, herbs, coffee, tea, cannabis. It was a notion which might make commercial

48

sense: though there were cheaper fully synthesised equivalents of all of these supplements, there was also an abiding nostalgia for anything seen as 'the genuine article', on a world where such things were intrinsically scarce. But there had been no sign that anything was happening with the complex beyond basic maintenance, for all that Jethro Xu had been here longer than a year already, and for all that it seemed likely a Xu elder would possess the material reserves to do much more with the buildings. That part of it made no sense, and it bothered Cory.

The image on Xu's office wall bothered him more, still rankled after his supposed rest: what was he to make of the implied history between Xu's daughter; the bland-looking young man whom Cory was fairly certain was Laith; and that third, too-familiar figure?

He was given more time to mull this after awakening, after breakfast, when Portia and Jethro Xu conversed in private for ten minutes or so, behind the office's sealed door. A credit transfer, most probably. Then Cory was admitted to the office, because the discussion had evidently progressed from commerce to something which concerned him directly: the operating specifications of the submersible which Portia was hiring, or purchasing, or had purchased, from Xu. As Portia's questions to Xu continued, things fell into place for Cory: he could now see, at last, the connections between the several items of piecework for which Portia had contracted his services, these past months back in Levin.

The submersible was to be crewed. It required enhancements to its life support systems, to its propulsion, to its heat engineering. It was clear now, though, from Xu's responses, that several of the specifications which Portia had provided to Cory, and which had guided the modding and the interface prep and the systems configuration which he'd undertaken for her in Levin, were not genuinely descriptive of the submersible's properties. In most instances the discrepancies were minor, but two important measures— the wattage of the radioisotope thermoelectric generator, the waste heat of which would need to be shepherded and dissipated, and the capacity of the cryopumps which were crucial to the operation of the vessel's propulsion system—were substantially different than the values he'd been given, the values on which he'd relied. The realisation both gutted and angered him, especially in view of Portia's earlier insistence that the specs were beyond reproach: he felt as though he'd been tricked into delivering substandard goods, he'd failed to do his best work. Listening to the back-and-forth between this strangely driven and secretive woman and their tall, reclusive host, and occasionally raising questions himself, Cory mapped the submersible's newly disclosed characteristics onto the operating specifications of the modules he'd crafted. They would still function as required, he thought, but the tolerances weren't there; and he had not perceived, until now, that the sum of his code and his componentry would need to keep a human safe under conditions wherein the smallest error would lead, with almost complete certitude, to an agonising death in helpless isolation. He'd known, the whole time, that it had been foolishness to have agreed to what Portia had euphemistically described as a fieldwork assignment, but he had not known the size of it. Now he found himself wondering whether it might be possible to arrange a lift back to Levin, or at least to Hörst, with Braun. But the woman from Soderblom pol was not in evidence this morning. Had she left already?

How long would it take him to walk to Cottini, through the foreboding velvet chill of a Titan farside night?

It wasn't truly an option, and he knew it. Not because of the distance involved, but because of what it would demand of him. Besides, were he to leave now, he would likely never get an explanation for why Jethro Xu's office displayed a portrait of Xu's daughter, taken five years ago in the company of Arum and her supposedly more recent lover.

He would also be cutting the final connection to his aunt, of whose death he'd learnt only three days ago.

All in all, he couldn't do it.

'You were very quiet in there,' Portia commented, as they found their way back to the smaller, less unpleasantly scented cafeteria. The statement wasn't an accusation, exactly, but it spoke nonetheless of judgment and disappointment.

Cory answered in the same vein. 'There was a bit much that I was hearing for the first time,' he said, his first words measured and even-tempered. 'Things I shouldn't have been hearing for the first time. Considering I've already spent—what is it?—certainly at least several weeks solid on this project, more likely a couple of months. You are never straight with me, you have not been straight with me from the outset, and even when I think you're being straight with me, even when it comes to parameters and operating requirements for the mods for this submersible's systems—things it's obviously well in both our interests to have correct, true, and unambiguous—even then there's misinformation and misdirection. Lies. I mean, first it's one version and then it's another, and then it's just a bit further along, not in this settlement, we'll get to where we need to finish up in the next settlement, and then another day, and then the next version, the next supposed destination, and then this Kalpana Braun comes out and asks you point-blank what's the truth, and you tell her this story about the submersible, and yes I believe the submersible, because I've seen it now, and I've heard the details from Xu, but the only thing, the only fucking thing I can be sure of in all of this is that the story you spun Braun and Xu, about us looking for part of an old spacecraft in one of the lakes, it's all just another lie in an ongoing series—'

'It happens to be the truth,' said Portia, pulling out a C-fibre chair so it scraped on the cafeteria's polymer decking. She sat down, beckoned for him to join her. 'Even if it omits important details.'

'And again! It's missing important details!' He remained standing. 'What do you mean, 'important details'?'

'While we're here, I'll keep that to myself. Xu comes across as trustworthy, and we'd get nowhere without his submersible, but someone knew our plans—Prof's plans—for Ontario Lacus. While the details of that breach are unclear, I want to avoid making the same mistake twice.'

'I think I can answer that,' said Cory. 'Xu's daughter has pharmhand connections. That must be how the ambushers were informed.'

'How do you work that?'

'That photo in his office. It's of Xu's daughter, right? She's in it with Arum and Laith.'

'Laith?'

'Friend of— doesn't matter,' said Cory, choosing not to explore further, for now, the datum that Arum's name had not been news to Portia. Something Teresa Maria had said to her, he supposed. 'So one of them most likely passed the intel along to that crew Braun was in with. In fact, Braun herself might be aware of some of the details. Were any of them here the previous time, when you and Whirr— you and this professor—'

'Wiremu,' said Portia.

'When you and Wiremu hired the other submersible from Xu?'

'No,' said Portia. 'No, it was just Xu here that time. And your aunt was with us by then. You're right, that does explain how the pharmhands down south might have known.'

'Only if Xu had been in contact with his daughter.'

'He speaks as though he is. But in any case, that doesn't change anything here, now.'

'Least of all that I was given the wrong specs for all the coding I've done for this,' said Cody, finally taking a seat. 'I don't know what it is you're chasing, and I'm past caring. I want the lot, or I'm out.'

'The lot?'

'The full story,' said Cory, 'or the full amount. And since you apparently have ongoing difficulty in providing the full story, I would say that leaves us with my other seventy percent. I'd like that now.'

'That is no way to do business,' said Portia.

'Neither is this,' he replied, splaying his palms apart facing her. 'If you want my continued assistance, and frankly I would say you'll need it, if those mods are so crucial to what you're trying to do, then you need to settle with me, here, now.'

'The agreement was for the remaining seventy percent on completion.'

'Was. And I don't think you can really pretend you've adhered to best practice. I'll continue with this, with nothing owing to me, or I won't continue.' He shook his head slightly, stared.

She met his stare, breathed deeply. Opened her mouth, closed it. Turned her head to the right, as though some answer lay in that direction. 'Agreed,' she said finally.

Damn, thought Cory.

four

'This Wiremu,' Cory said, then hesitated. 'How close were you?'

It was difficult to hear him over the Duck's throaty rumble. The vehicle was negotiating the rutted track that led from Xu's hermitage to the main trackway and thence to Cottini. The track was, in truth, more a notion now than a coherent actuality, due to an amalgam of neglect and floodplain drainage. Not that it presented the Duck any insuperable difficulty.

Portia had kept the cab cold, the way she liked it. If Cory was planning to interfere with the temperature controls, he kept such aspirations to himself.

Outside the Duck, it was deep in full night, such a starless commodity as only Farside could serve up. The settlement, a handful of kilometres distant, was not directly visible beyond the interposed ridge of stained ice. Cottini's location, nonetheless, could be approximately identified on the basis of hazeshine: a deep-grey smudge, high ahead, that could sporadically be seen despite the bouncing glare of the Duck's headlights. The way was illuminated, too, by the navigation drone which Portia had deployed and which now tracked above the Duck's path, augmenting the visual and radar detail on the uneven and unpredictable terrain encountered by the Duck. She could have called up an overlay on the windscreen, to provide locational information and other metrics for her and Cory, but she preferred to keep things minimal.

It was good to be travelling at night. It felt safer to have left Xu's, to have swapped its sometimes problematic air for the Duck's, and to have left behind Xu's equally problematic familial connections. She didn't want too much cluttering that fragile feeling of escape or release; there was enough else going on for her. Was she ready for what lay ahead? She had rehearsed anticlimax so many times, over the past months; but there was, still, no way of knowing.

It had taken three daycycles camped at Xu's halfheartedly refurbished facility before Cory apparently felt that he had adapted or reconstructed the mods and the purpose-built componentry sufficiently to work with the submersible. It had been time they didn't really have. Portia had fretted it out; she didn't see that there had been any choice. The submersible needed to function. There was nothing substantive which she could do to assist with this; it was Cory's expertise she was relying on now, and much as she struggled with the delay, she was nonetheless heartened by the enthusiasm, still, with which he threw himself at each small but seemingly intractable problem. (She'd been able to do that herself once, had earned and indeed deserved Prof's esteem as an inexhaustible and inventive researcher, but it grew more difficult to sustain that cautiously optimistic tirelessness the older you got, the more setbacks you notched up.) Watching Cory make slow but definite progress with the tasks required, she began to feel more sure that Teresa Maria had not steered her wrong in talking up his abilities. She hoped he was indeed every bit as proficient as his reputation promised, as his focus now suggested; they could not afford errors. It was important to ensure that everything tested out correctly, before they even contemplated immersion in the lethally chilled methane-ethane-nitrogen mix of a Titan sea. She'd been angry at Xu for having earlier provided her with the wrong specifications to the submersible, but really the fault lay as much with her as with him. She should have queried why, if the two submersibles were so substantially different in design, they had had the same specs...

But it was sorted now, or so she hoped. There was just whatever they were heading towards; and Cory's question. She'd taken her time to prepare a response, but still didn't know if she had the sum of it. It had been five years of a closer-than-most professional relationship; it wasn't an easy thing to quantify.

'We weren't lovers, if that's what you were inquiring about,' she said.

'It wasn't,' said Cory, seeming to stifle a yawn. Well, he'd put in long hours; she wasn't going to begrudge him his fatigue.

'Wiremu was more like family to me,' said Portia. 'Although there was the supervisory aspect to the relationship too, of course. Not that that ever became too apparent; he was good at valuing my feedback, and at giving the impression that I was in charge of the day-to-day aspects of our work. Which was as it should be, I suppose, since it was generally my hands on the instruments.' She fell into reverie, thinking of that time three or four years ago, on the ekranoplan, when it had looked as though they were going to die. How bittersweet, to have survived that, as though they were invincible; and then Ontario Lacus, where she had survived only by the accident of being closeted and asleep at the time.

'I don't think I've heard anyone else speak about a supervisor in such terms,' said Cory, after several seconds. 'Colleagues, sometimes, perhaps, but the management role never struck me as one that brought out any particularly positive characteristics in people. This should not be taken as a comment on any of my clients, of course.'

'Noted,' said Portia, attempting a wry smile. She dabbed at her eyes.

'But you have family still,' he stated.

'Technically, yes,' she replied. 'But they're in—what is it they call it now?—public perceptions engineering. We both agree that what each other is doing is a waste of time, so I have as little to do with them as possible.'

'I don't get that option,' said Cory.

It was a complaint, plain enough, but not primarily directed against her; at least, she chose that interpretation. She let the statement stand without response. It wasn't something with which she could help him, and she was wary of making matters worse between herself and him again.

'There's a further favour I need to ask of you,' she said a few minutes later, as the Duck registered a complaint at the upslope it was facing.

When he didn't answer, she continued. 'I have business in Cottini. So I will need to stop there for a daycycle or two, to sort some details. But there are aspects of the submersible's field testing that cannot wait for that. Therefore, I need you to take the Duck on ahead, to Vänern.'

'Vänern? Not Ligeia?'

She mused; bit her tongue as the Duck bumped through a pothole on the track's left edge. In response, she upped the drone's gain. 'Vänern, yes. Smaller lake, shallower, it's just a better environment for testing. I'll join you as soon as I can.'

'How? I'll have the Duck.'

'I'll hire something portable at Cottini. A skid-bike, a powered sled. A thopter, if need be.'

'I don't know the way to Vänern from here,' Cory complained.

'The Duck knows,' she said, a little dismissively. They'd crested the ridge; the Duck angled downslope, and the squat illuminated drum of Cottini was visible directly ahead, an improbable high-contrast blue intrusion against the dun ice and the surrounding darkness. 'You'll get there with no problems. I've already prepped a listing of the tests you'll need to put the submersible through when you get there. Beyond that, I have trust in your ingenuity.' Then there was something said which she could have sworn she had not uttered aloud, something which would have been at most sotto voce; but somehow, in the general rumble and buzz of the Duck's cab, Cory picked up on it anyway.

'Kraken. You said Vänern before, and then Ligeia.' His tone was accusatory.

'I didn't say Ligeia.'

'Back at Xu's you did. See, this is more of what I've been complaining about.'

'Ligeia was necessary misdirection, among people I couldn't treat as entirely trustworthy. Vänern's the proving ground. Three days of field tests. Then on to Kraken.'

'Why the hell should I believe Kraken, when all your previous iterations have turned out to be fake?'

'Cory, I've had to be careful with what information I reveal. Ontario Lacus drummed that into me. Hire a submersible, and everyone thinks there's only one kind of thing you could be looking for, and therefore that what you're doing must be lucrative, or at least potentially so. That's the thinking which got Wiremu and Teresa Maria killed.'

'I get that. Which is why I think I have shown some patience on this. But you said Ligeia was about the search for an early probe heat shield. That's at least plausible; but I'm guessing it hasn't somehow found its way to Kraken instead. So if it's not the heat shield, what the fuck is this?'

She took her time answering, which she covered by calling the navigation drone back to its dock. With the lights foregrounding Cottini, the drone had diminished to become just another moving part, and it was always best to risk as few of those as possible.

One side of Portia, the side which still remembered the frisson of discovery, was almost ready to tell Cory the truth. The tension which this provoked in her unnerved her. She had to do this without unnecessary errors, and disclosure remained in that category, even now. She settled for something, at least, which wasn't a lie. 'If I find it, I promise you, you'll be the first to know. I owe you that.'

'Which means what?'

'Nothing lucrative, nothing valuable. Potentially nothing at all. I'd say the chances on that are fairly high. But it's something I have to try. For Wiremu.'

He seemed to accept that; at least, his questions took a more practical turn. 'How do we get from Vänern to Kraken? That'd have to be a hell of an overland route. Ligeia we could reach in, what, a day or two from Vänern. Kraken would have to be five or six, or more because I'm guessing there isn't any kind of trail there from here.'

'There is a trail, but it's not exactly vehicle-friendly. Don't worry, I have that sorted.'

'Which means what?'

'I'm not going overland.'

'I? Not we?'

59

She held up her hand as a 'wait' signal while her earpiece received parking directions from Cottini traffic control. Not that she expected anything approaching congestion; her understanding was that the settlement only ever filled up twice a decade or so, when for two weeks it hosted the regional prospectors' convention.

She was busy for the next couple of minutes, responding to the official and guiding the Duck to its isolated berth in the short-stay parking bay. Traffic control advised that an airlock vehicle had been dispatched for her convenience. She signed off. Turned to the contractor sitting beside her. 'Cory, I can't ask that of you. I've paid you out, I've bought your time for the three days of field tests at Vänern. But I can't afford more than that, and that's the truth.'

'So I've sunk all this time into this mysterious project, and I'm not even going to be there when you do the main dive in Kraken?'

'Main dives. Series of main dives in Kraken. Potentially quite a few.'

'I don't see that that changes anything.'

'It's a big body. Like I said, there's a good probability I won't find anything. Even if I do, I might need weeks. Months.'

That, she hoped, would be the end of it. She stood up and walked back to her berth, set about packing. But Cory apparently needed more. He followed her as she packed, was careful not to encroach on her personal space—no small achievement that, in the Duck's cramped interior—but made it plain that the conversation was not complete.

'Months?' he asked. 'For what?'

five

It was night, and would be so for several daycycles yet. The darkness gripped him like a clamp.

The night mood was always a challenge; but back in Levin, where this unease had formed only a backdrop to the ongoing work or to the hours of rest and domestic routine, matters had been busy enough, and sufficiently populated, that it was possible to devalue the mood, to discount the memories it churned up. Traversing the hinterlands of northern farside Titan with Portia, in the Duck, it had also been straightforward—for the most part—for Cory to ignore the threats of which the darkness spoke. Solitude was different; solitude sharpened the sense of precariousness.

It was not a fear of the dark itself, exactly, but of what the dark might conceal. It was, he knew, a largely irrational concern—this desolate shore was not the contested expanse between Ponnamperuna and Neimann, where Dayani and Lex had lost their lives, and where he had very nearly joined them—but this knowledge held little power, in the absence of light and of companionship. Vänern's night-shrouded, tholin-stained ice-gravel beach; the low-lying blanket of hydrocarbon fog that lay over the lake's chill surface; the comprehensive sense of isolation in a setting where no sign of settlement or habitation was visible, save those he had brought here himself: the Duck, its trailer, the beached submersible, the prefab outbuilding which he had unpacked and inflated soon after arrival, himself. There had not even been any signs of older vehicle tracks, though he found it difficult to believe this particular spot had not seen previous visitors; Vänern, as one of the lower-latitude and more readily accessible among the northern polar regions' plentiful lakes, would surely be likely to see campers and amateur explorers during the well-lit summer years. Perhaps they were an uncharacteristically tidy lot, who'd left no detritus.

To begin with, there had been plenty to attend to: ensuring the newly inflated outbuilding's layer of argonogel insulation had cured properly; testing the outbuilding's airlocks; stowing the project's gear, tools, and instruments within the temporary building's workspace, in readiness for any necessary repairs or further modifications to the submersible; preparing for the first lake trial of the vessel. The submersible itself, too large to fit within the outbuilding's confines, would stay where he had unloaded it, on a hydrocarbon-sedimented ice-gravel beach from which he hoped it would be straightforward to push into Vänern's cripplingly cold shallows. Having experienced the sediment's slightly spongy response to the weight of his T-suit boots, Cory wasn't fully convinced it would be possible to gain sufficient traction for the task to succeed; but that would be a challenge for the following daycycle. He had grown too tired, and too hungry, to contemplate further exertion for tonight.

The outbuilding lacked windows, and this was a point in its favour. Though it was possible to opacify the Duck's windscreen, to do so could not dispel the sense that something was out there, waiting in the long darkness; it was somehow easier, in the outbuilding, to simply pretend that there was no beyond, or so he hoped.

The prefab unit's accom section stank of plasticiser and of the piss-like scent of spilled insulation when he cracked his T-suit's helmet seal, and the cold hit him shortly thereafter. He shucked the suit, climbed into thick thermals, and set about unfolding the hard decking which would form an additional layer of insulation underfoot, lifting first one double-moccasined foot and then the other off the decking while he did so. The unit would eventually warm up to something approaching comfort, but it was taking its time in doing so. He selected the spiciest of the available ready-prepareds, in the hope that it might assist with his own thermal management.

If it did, the effect was transitory.

Sleep, as expected, took its time.

A boot slammed into his back; hands scrabbled to remove the nightsuit's air supply. The weight of another's suit pinning him prone and helpless against the dirty ice surface. The burnt-metal-and-bleach sharpness of Titan, finding its way in through the breach in his suit; the knowledge of death's imminence, before even panic had had a chance to muster.

Cory woke, heart thudding, his skin mapped in beads of quick-chilled sweat. The location was unrecognisable, and it was only once logic had had an opportunity to reboot in his abruptly awakened state that he could work it out: the accom unit, with his T-suit, discarded like a reptile's sloughed skin, piled in the inflatable hab's solid-framed airlock. He searched out the status panel, did not entirely believe its reassuring green glow. Over a couple of minutes, his breathing slowed and shallowed to a more comfortable rhythm.

He checked the chrono. He'd had only half his customary sleep, but the prospect of attempting to rest further did not appeal.

The notion of donning his T-suit and exiting the hab to go through the submersible's buoyancy test didn't much appeal either, but it was what was needful.

The airlock was cold, even by the accom unit's standards. He pulled the T-suit into the hab's main room and powered up the warming pads in the suit's lining, ignoring the Titan tang rising from the bootsoles while he went to see what would serve for breakfast.

It was never the actions of his aunt that he dreamt about, though those had been traumatic as she fought to plumb into his suit the air supply she'd wrenched off Lex's back. This was something which resurfaced repeatedly in his walking mind: that Teresa Maria had quite literally saved his life within moments of learning of Lex's death. It would have been natural had she resented his survival in some way, as a continuing reminder of her lover's death; and yet as far as he could recall, there had been no resentment or bitterness towards him. A sense of darkness, sure, even some kind of doom which hovered around her; but that could just be, on his part, an unfamiliarity with the depths of grief, since he had been too young to remember his mother's loss and had not really lost anyone truly close (except in the fundamentally different sense in which he'd lost Arum) until, just a week ago now, he had belatedly learnt of Teresa Maria's death. To think on such things—and it seemed to happen unpredictably, sometimes unwillingly—was to apply a brake to his capabilities, to untether himself in some fashion, to cause everything to spiral back towards the crux of danger and assault and his own near-death, and for these reasons he tried not to dwell on such matters. But it happened, nonetheless.

The long nights didn't help.

He hit a difficulty with the buoyancy testing. Assisted by his T-suit's servos, he had managed to push the submersible, like some oversized turtle, into Vänern's shallows; was able to test out the vessel's basic functions through commands transmitted via the three fizzing warmed-cable hawsers which kept it moored ten metres offshore; had performed some carefully contained checks of its propulsion system; could not persuade it to descend beneath the surface. At first he'd believed the problem to be too much residual warmth in the ballast tanks, causing the methane to boil, but though the craft settled slightly after a time, it still would not sink on command. He ran through what he could recollect of the vessel's specifications, then called up the manual itself on his helmet's HUD. Eventually he realised that the submersible needed an occupant. Without its payload of a seventy-kilogram human, its C-fibre hull was simply too low in density. And Vänern's liquid was low-density: fractionally warmer, nitrogen-poor, more methane-rich and less perfused by denser ethane than was that of deep and ancient Kraken. If the submersible would not sink, when required, in Vänern, then it certainly would not manage to do so in the larger body which was its ultimate destination. He hauled the craft back in towards the shore, straining at the exertion and crimping one of the tethering cables beyond the prospect of re-use, while he tried to think how best to address the problem. Portia was not here, and while it would have been possible for him to clamber into the beached submersible's cramped cockpit, refloat the vessel, and test it out from within, it went against all safety principles to attempt such an action. An alternative remedy was needed.

Was there a sufficient mass of equipment on hand, in the accom unit and the outbuilding, to simulate the crew's weight? He supposed there was, but it was going to be cumbersome to assemble, and to load. Not that there was really any choice.

There were two aspects of the submersible's operation with which he was intrinsically dissatisfied, regardless of any issues of performance. One was the airlock, which was necessarily highly confined, more or less just a minimum-width horizontal cylindrical chamber accessed from a rectangular hatch in the vessel's roof. Once within the airlock, it was impossible for the submersible's occupant to access sufficient freedom of movement, not even of her helmet. From the airlock, it was basically necessary to fall into the cockpit, and this main chamber represented the vessel's other design failing, in Cory's eyes. The cockpit was, for no structural reason which he could discern, significantly too narrow and too tight to accommodate a lakesuited occupant, even someone wearing one of the high-end Reynolds/Volker Project slimline immersion suits, and was certainly off-limits to anyone in a more routinely affordable standard lakesuit such as that which Portia owned. It meant she would need to wear her general-purpose T-suit, which made for somewhat greater manoeuvreability but which offered significantly poorer thermal protection against the deep cryogenic chill of Vänern, or of Kraken. This would make any dive both more uncomfortable and more dangerous than it properly should be: were any malfunction to occur, even in close proximity to the shore, the T-suit might not give Portia enough opportunity to reach safety.

Cory's concerns at these features had been acknowledged by Portia, but she had let him know that she believed the potential gains of the project—whatever those might be—justified the dangers. It wasn't his place, she informed him, to seek to limit her actions out of fear for her safety. She placed sufficient trust in the submersible's design and construction, and in the modifications they had worked on, to risk descending to one of the deepest stretches within all of Titan's chilled lakes and seas. He still didn't truly understand the purpose of the dive or dives, but that wasn't his place either.

All of this was running, like firmware, through his mind while he balanced awkwardly beside the hull's open hatch, wondering how best to load the polymer sacks of clothing and ready-prepareds and miscellaneous gear into the submersible's airlock and then to remotely drop them into the cockpit beneath. The airlock itself was too cramped to allow him to climb in with any of the polymer sacks and to tamp it into the confined space; in the end he settled for repeatedly using each successive sack to jostle those loaded earlier, effecting a crude and inefficient redistribution of the items within the almost-inaccessible space. There was something vaguely peristaltic about it; he hoped the buffeting had not cracked any of the ready-prepareds' casings. Then there was a major difficulty in closing the hatch; but it was done. He exited the airlock, returned to the accom unit for lunch: while he could have chosen from the suit's stowed rations, he needed to shuck his carapace for a while.

The test descent worked: he succeeded, through flooding the ballast tanks, in inducing the submersible to sink to the lake's bed just offshore. It was no great depth, barely three metres at that point, but it sufficed to ensure that the vessel was fully immersed, with a layer of languidly fizzing liquid covering the hatch as the lake's liquid methane absorbed the heat of the craft's operations. It was a satisfactory first step, but the sight of the vessel sinking beneath the surface left him with misgivings. The next time it descended, it would be crewed.

He was progressing as best he could with the task of extracting the polymer sacks from the cockpit of the beached vessel—this was a difficulty he should have anticipated, but hadn't—when he heard an extraneous mechanical sound. He hastened to complete the job, hurriedly closed the hatch. There was a skid-bike, an ancient Hainan twin-seater, parked aslant on the tholin-stained gravel, its kickstand sunken partway into a gap between the pebbles of ice. Portia had returned.

She wasn't alone, though. It seemed she had been given a lift. At first he thought the second individual, still-T-suited and bending to place Portia's carryall beside the accom unit's airlock, was the pol woman from Soderblom, Bloom or Brown or something—Braun—but a closer look at the suit, as the figure straightened and turned, indicated it could not be her. The build was wrong, as was the suit's body language.

It was Arum.

Portia's surprise at the recognition which passed between Cory and Arum appeared genuine; he would explore that later. For now, there was the shock of Arum's presence, the conflict it awoke within him. How was she here, when she had announced she was moving offworld, to Rhea or Mimas? What was her purpose? He didn't believe at all that this meeting could be accidental. And what of Laith?

He seized what initiative he could. 'Can we talk?' he asked. A look from Portia, as she turned her helmet towards Cory, he took for assent; Arum's response was less straightforwardly decipherable. No matter. 'Back soon,' he added, brightening his suit's fog-lamps and gesturing along the direction of the shoreline. Arum took his cue, and they set off southeast, keeping a few metres from the dark liquid's rim and cutting through pale tendrils of hydrocarbon mist as they walked.

'I thought it was Mimas,' he said. Left the statement hanging.

'Wait,' she said, stopping. He paused. She turned to him, lifting her gloves towards either side of his helmet, holding them against it for a few seconds before lifting them away. An incongruously tender gesture; an appropriation; an intrusion. Something in his HUD shifted, slid sideways and then restored itself. 'Now we can talk,' she explained. They resumed walking.

'I don't think that was necessary,' he said.

'Then we differ. I'll give you the uninstall passcode after. I know very little about your friend, but—'

'She's my employer.'

'That doesn't matter to me. What she is is an unknown quantity, and I need to be careful about who I'm speaking with.'

'I don't want to be a part of whatever this is,' he said. 'I just want to know why you're here.'

'Same,' she replied. 'You asked about Mimas. They contacted me two days before I was due to lift. Told me they would restore details to my record which I had been careful to sanitise, unless I cooperated. I couldn't take the chance.'

'And so you're here now.'

'You think I want this?'

'I've no idea anymore, not since I saw that pic at Jethro Xu's complex.'

'Pic?'

'You, Laith, and Xu's daughter. Not particularly recent, but that hardly matters, does it?'

'Cory, I—' She stopped again, turned away from him. Inspected the mist-sheeted expanse of Vänern. 'That's past, I swear. I just need something to give them, so they will hopefully leave me alone.'

No need, he thought, *to ask who 'they' were.* 'And then what?'

'What do you mean?'

'When they leave you alone, what will you do? Mimas again?'

'No, I think it's safest not. At least for a while. I have work arranged, starting after the next day/night cycle. It's clean, and it's a long way from here. It's best you don't know more than that.'

'Whereas you apparently want to know everything.'

'Not true. I just need enough to give them.'

'So why didn't you ask Portia on the ride over? She knows far more about this than I do.'

'You know I couldn't do that. I don't have a history with her. And she'd wonder why I was asking. Besides, I know she'll have told you some, and there are other parts you'll have figured out yourself.'

'She'll wonder why she doesn't hear anything if she's trying to listen in on this.'

'Oh, she'll hear something,' said Arum. 'It just won't be this conversation.'

'What will— look, I don't really care. But I don't see why I need to help you out here.'

'I can't provide that reason for you. I'm just asking for enough to be able to pass on to them, to explain matters. Because they see a submersible, they see people involved who have previously attacked their kind—and that's both you and this Portia, the way they read things— and they see secrecy and misdirection, and I suppose they need to know if they need to adopt... active measures to dissuade whatever this is. I don't know. Maybe they're concerned you'll go probing in the wrong lake, that wouldn't entirely surprise me. Or maybe they think Portia, or you, has the location of a sunken ore-rich lode. I know for sure Vänern isn't the main goal.'

Cory made a choice then. Perhaps it had been the mod Arum had gimmicked into his suit's comms system; perhaps he would have made the same decision regardless. It hardly seemed to matter. 'I've been told it's Ligeia,' he said, took a long sip from the suit's water nipple. 'Portia thinks she has the approximate resting place of one of the larger components from one of the early unmanned-probe Titan exploration missions. The heat shield, I think.' He paused for another mouthful of water. 'I honestly don't know any more than that. And I don't see why it would be any kind of big deal—I suppose, yeah, it has cultural significance, and there's probably one of the big museums in Sagan or Kuiper or Coustenis which would include it and display it in their collection, but I don't think it'd have any significant commercial value. I mean, it's not the probe itself, it's just a slab of metal.'

'What kind of metal?' asked Arum. 'You know how overcooked the local ore market is, and how pricy it is to import asteroidal ore.'

'Yes, but… a historically significant artefact like that? There'd be an uproar if someone smelted it for, I don't know, its nickel content or whatever. And I don't honestly know what kind, I haven't asked. My guess would be something lightweight, like aluminium and maybe a ceramic layer, because back then they were stingy with boost for anything sent out this far. But I mean, that would be on the record somewhere, you could probably call it up now if you're curious.'

'That's really what this is about? It sounds… thin. For this amount of effort, I mean.'

'It's what I've been told,' said Cory cautiously. 'Is it enough to pass on to… them?'

'If it's really the deal, it'll have to be.'

He didn't reply, gazed out instead at what was visible of the lake's almost wax-smooth surface beneath the low-lying skeins of mist. Wondered how far out the lamps on his suit could actually illuminate. There was no end to the lake; and Vänern Lacus was not particularly large, not as such bodies went.

'What are you thinking?' she asked.

'Such a calm surface,' he replied. 'It's intimidating, in a way.'

'Don't,' she said, without explaining what it was she was advising him against. 'Just don't. You won't fix anything brooding on the past.'

'Who said anything about the past?'

'I know you. Just because what we had was broken in some ways doesn't mean I don't know the way your mind works.'

'I honestly don't think I was I was thinking that.' He stooped down and plucked an ice pebble from the shore, its evaporite crusting greasy in the fugitive warmth from his glove. He stretched his arm back and flung the pebble lakeward. The suit's servos imparted a more than human-capable velocity to the projectile; in the mist and darkness, he failed to detect its trajectory in his lamps' beams. The pebble was just gone, no distant splash of impact discernible against the soft mechanical noise of the suit, the biomechanical murmur of its occupant, the transmitted sounds of his neighbour. The mystery of the pebble's fate was somehow more intimidating than the unguessable limits of the lake itself: it was as if he had thrown a rock into some creature's lair and was now awaiting its emergence. 'We should be getting back,' he announced.

'Should we?'

'You've got what you came for.'

'Have I?'

'You're the one who warned against brooding on the past.'

'I did,' she said. 'And I'm not. I just don't think you are telling me everything.'

'I have told you what I've been told. You're welcome to try getting more out of Portia yourself.'

'We both know that won't happen. And yes, you have passed on what you know. Or some of it. But this heat shield? I found its details in less than a minute, just now, and yes, it's mostly aluminium. No significant value, in terms of ore content. Dubious historical value too, for that matter. You could have found that information too, as quickly and as easily. What bothers me is that you didn't. And yet you expect me to believe this is the goal of your mysterious quest.'

'It's not my mysterious quest,' he replied. 'It's Portia's mysterious quest. I really am not that curious. I just need to know that the submersible is capable of operating as it needs to.'

'But part of knowing what it needs to be capable of is knowing what it's seeking. It was such an easy thing to check, but you apparently hadn't; and yet you tend to be detail-focussed. I think there's something you're not telling me.'

'I— There isn't anything I'm not telling you.'

She was silent for several seconds, her visor turned away from his field of view. 'You're right, we should be getting back. The passcode is Karasi.'

'Pardon me?'

She repeated the word.

'And is that supposed to mean anything of significance?' he asked. He had started to follow her back, parallel to the shoreline. The lights of the accom unit were dim, fog-smudged, not seeming at any particular distance. Their earlier bootprints in the gravelly ice were sporadically discernible along the way ahead as small pools of transient shadow.

'It's the name of a family friend, when I was growing up in Neimann. She moved to Sagan when I was seven. I missed her for months. Nothing of significance other than that.'

He fell silent. The passcode was a marker that their private conversation was done, and with it any chance of exploring aspects of their shared past. He hadn't wished to do so, but resisted the implication that he was now barred from such possibilities. The walk back was defined, in the same way that the outward walk had been undefined. There was a set destination.

Arum was problematic, but he would miss her. He would miss this, whatever 'this' was. What there had been between him and Arum had once seemed ideal, or as near to ideal as could be wished, before he had learnt that there were things about her, about them, which he had needed to explain away or to ignore if he wished to maintain that pretence of ideality.

He had so wished. He'd continued to wish it, up to and beyond the point of needing to decide whether to stay aligned to his aunt, who had saved his life, or to his lover, whom Teresa Maria palpably had not trusted.

It had been a useless choice, badly made; he'd lost both.

He uttered the passcode. There was no reason not to, and he would forget if he waited too long. There *were* things he wished to say, but he did not. And then they were back at the accom unit.

She stayed only long enough to afford Portia another opportunity to thank her for providing the transport; then she was gone, with a growl of the skid-bike's engine and an ostentatious spray of ice pebbles.

*

'She still means something important to you,' Portia suggested to him after Arum's departure.

He made a noise which he hoped sounded noncommittal, even indifferent. In truth, he didn't know where he stood, not with Arum, not with Portia herself, not with the shape of his own life.

They were in the accom unit, unsuited, eating a hastily chosen meal. It was more difficult to dissemble when one's face wasn't shielded by a visor. Not that he wanted to dissemble, but nor did he want to be probed. All in all, it wasn't a conversation he wished to have, not with someone for whom he'd just lied to his former lover, not with someone from whom he still hadn't received a straight answer yet, so far as he could establish, to his own questions. Instead, he briefed her on the outcome of the submersible's initial lake trial. It was what he was paid for, after all. She was eager to try a crewed test as soon as they had finished the meal. This went against his instincts for caution, but she wouldn't be dissuaded.

If she had further questions about his discussion with Arum, they stayed unspoken amidst all the preparations for launch. Cory found himself wondering whether his suit's comms remained compromised in some way, from whatever piece of patchware Arum had passed to his helmet. He wanted to believe the passcode had unravelled it utterly, but he couldn't afford to take that on trust. It would take time to check the suit's digital hygiene; he didn't have that time just now, with all the checks which needed performing on the submersible, and he could not suggest a delay for that purpose without alerting Portia to Arum's efforts to conceal their conversation from her. Later, it would have to be later, while in the meantime he took care with his statements and strove not to lose focus on what was a demanding and crucial set of technical tasks. Portia, for her part, was visibly keyed up at the prospect of testing out the submersible; she was, he thought, more animated by this than he had seen her before. It was as though she could almost just reach out and grab the object which she had sought for so long, the thing which wasn't in Vänern and which wasn't a century-plus-old heat shield and to which they would need to travel by some as-yet-undisclosed means regarding which she had told him not to worry.

It still made no sense. Whatever she sought, surely it was not worth this effort. This expense. This excitement. This paranoid secrecy.

This risk.

They reviewed the outline for the crewed test, suited up, and went outside to the lakeshore to set up.

The test went well. Perhaps whatever it was Portia was embarked upon would not be a complete disaster.

She was in a strange mood following the crewed immersion trial. On edge, or keyed up; he couldn't decide which. They were—or so he thought—going about their separate preparations for sleep, with the meal table now converted into two lightweight fabric-and-frame cots, when she cleared her throat.

'Thank you for covering for me,' she told him. 'With Arum'.

He raised his eyebrow, waiting to see what followed.

'Goodnight, Cory,' she said. That was all, apparently.

He woke early, conscious that something unidentifiable had changed. Portia was sleeping soundly; it felt slightly invasive to remain more-or-less fully awake in her presence, and a return to sleep was not on the menu. He rose, dressed, donned his airlock-cold T-suit, exited the prefab.

There were lights on Vänern, something he initially thought was a wall or a building. After a few seconds his brain caught up enough for identification purposes.

It was a flying boat, an old Mitsuda Mark 2 Wavecutter if he wasn't mistaken, in the livery of one of the major freight concerns and anchored perhaps two or three hundred metres offshore. It must have been the plane's descent which had awoken him. Approaching the shore from the Wavecutter there was a motorised barge, crewed by a T-suited figure who stood at the vessel's control station. When the barge grounded on the bay's gravelly shore, the figure dismounted and waded ashore in his direction.

The T-suit's occupant was compact; spare; female. 'You must be the nephew', she said, reaching Cory.

six

It was good to reconnect with Junko Shaw, though the pilot's schedule was sufficiently bereft of free time to do so properly; there was merely the opportunity for a T-suited hug, a brief exchange of mutual condolences. and then the necessity of loading everything aboard the big electroprop flying boat. She left Junko and Cory to an animated discussion of tonnages and the powered barge's laden weight capacity. This was a complication she had not planned for, because the expectation had been that Cory would take the Duck, and the hired trailer, back to Cottini while she was transported with the submersible and the re-stowed outbuilding to an island due north of Kraken's throat. Cory, however, had rebelled; had insisted it was necessary for him to accompany the submersible, had said it was lunacy to expect that a ten-metre practice dive in Vänern could in any sense be considered sufficient preparation for the very much deeper endurance dives which would be attempted in Kraken. So Cory was staying with her, which meant the Duck and the hired trailer needed to go with her too. Secretly she was pleased; the Duck and trailer would make much more straightforward the task of relocating her Kraken shoreside encampment, when or if that became necessary, and Cory's abilities at maintenance and repair could prove invaluable. But it complicated the financials in a way she didn't want to think about, because the trailer rental would continue to slowly ramp, because the on-sale of the Duck (which was to have been the last duty she assigned to Cory) would now need to be substantially delayed, and because even though she had stressed repeatedly to him that there was nothing more she could offer him by way of remuneration—a condition which he had accepted, for motivations she could not discern—he would still need to eat while out in the field, as would she. The five additional months' rations she had remotely purchased in Cottini, and which were already carried on the flying boat, would be gone inside three.

It couldn't be helped. There was no way of knowing whether three months would suffice for her to find what she sought; neither was there any way of knowing whether anything was there to seek. Three months must suffice; there wouldn't be a further chance.

She occupied herself with clearing out the accom unit before instigating its deflation. During the process of packing away Cory's effects—and she really had not been seeking to pry in the process— she found a small flat image, evidently of Arum. It wasn't her business. Nonetheless, it was somehow unsatisfying that the image was not instead of Teresa Maria, who had surely been much more steadfastly on his side, or even of the mother he had lost a decade and more before. *Just leave it*, she told herself, but it was difficult to do so.

Last to be bundled up was the polymer decking. Absent this additional insulation underfoot, the prefab unit's floor was almost cripplingly cold; she decided it was time to don the T-suit once more, though it felt vaguely ridiculous to be wearing it for moving within an interior space.

When all was ready, she moved as much of the baggage as was feasible into one of the airlocks, sealed it in, and then moved through to the other airlock, belatedly noticing that the gear in Cory's workspace had not yet been stowed. It would be better for him to attend to that. She exited the unit.

Cory and Junko had decided upon an order of operations. They would fill the trailer with the personal effects and other loose items, Cory would ride across on the barge with it, and would then remain onboard the plane, awaiting the Duck's arrival on the barge's next voyage, remotely manoeuvring it onto the landing stage and then driving it carefully into the flying boat's capacious cargo hold. They had evidently decided that the barge was just sufficiently buoyant to sustain the Duck's weight without sinking. (She hoped they had taken Vänern's low-density liquid into consideration in this calculation.) But she noted, aloud, that in any case the tools had not yet been stowed: they could surely be loaded aboard the submersible for the third and final voyage across to the plane, since without ballast the submersible was only a fraction of the Duck's weight, but didn't it therefore make more sense for her to go across with the trailer, instead, and to secure the Duck after it was sent across, while Cory stayed behind loading the tools into the submersible?

Cory allowed, cautiously, that that did make more sense, but it was clear he was somewhat disappointed in this outcome.

Moving the trailer onto the barge, and thence into the Mitsuda's cargo space, was problem-free. Junko showed her where to stand on the barge's deck, for optimal balance; the pilot narrated each operation as she performed it, so Portia would be competent at the task when the Duck was sent across unaccompanied. The most important aspects appeared to be a slow and steady barge velocity and a gradual braking manoeuvre, executed significantly before one would have judged it necessary. 'If you think you've left just enough distance for braking, you probably haven't,' was Junko's advice. 'We can make up some time in the air if we have to, but we need to get airborne first for that to happen. Slow is efficient, fast causes mistakes.'

You sound like Prof, thought Portia, though she was careful not to say it. Junko's tone might have been mothering, but she meant well; and she was helping them out tremendously by providing the transport. Portia hadn't expected her to agree, hadn't even expected a response to her request of several months back. But Junko had apparently accepted that there was some bond between them, the shared loss of Wiremu—not that Portia could really see how losing an ex-brother-in-law rated. Evidently it did, in this case. Or maybe the connection between her and the other woman was entirely separate from the relationship of each with Wiremu, but that, too, was hard to fathom. Prior to Ontario, Portia and Junko had spent perhaps five daycycles in each other's company, not more, spanning two flights and the preparations for same. It wasn't a lot; but, seemingly, it was enough. Portia felt safe and at ease in Junko Shaw's company, in a way which had taken much longer with others, even with Prof, or with Cory. With some of her colleagues such comfort had just never arrived. It was strange; and she was wary of analysing it too deeply.

The flying boat became a cave in front of them: rectangular, dark, tall, light-rimmed. As steady afloat as a building's foundations, unaffected even by the barge's approach.

Junko trimmed the barge's heading, nudged it slowly forward; there was an alarming graunching sensation from the barge's prow, to which Junko paid no particular heed, other than to cut the barge's motor. From this point, Portia gathered, momentum and the plane's loading mechanisms would take the barge properly onto the landing stage. After two minutes of gradual forward motion, the barge somehow locked itself in place; a tailgate swung up behind. There was a messily discordant eruption of low-pitched mechanical sound, and the barge began to rise, like a vessel in the locks which Portia vaguely recollected from a childhood holiday with her family in the lakes region, three-quarters of a Saturn year ago. Another mechanism engaged itself and the ascent stopped. A gate on the Mitsuda's cargo deck folded down, and then it was difficult to discern where the barge ended and the cargo deck began. Portia waited until Junko had stepped across whatever threshold there was; then she followed suit.

'Think you can manage that?' Junko asked her, the words precisely clipped, as she gestured back towards the barge. Portia nodded. Then watched, not really helping as much as she felt she ought, while the diminutive pilot winched the trailer through to the front of the cargo space and activated some feature in the decking which locked itself around the trailer's wheels, immobilising it. For good measure, Junko lashed it down with a trio of thick polymer chains, anchored into the deck.

With the plane immobile, it felt like overkill, but it would be good to know that things were thoroughly secure while they were in flight.

She waited in the cargo space for Junko, now back ashore, to send the Duck across. From the dialogue between Cory and the pilot, it sounded as though they were having problems ensuring that it was thoroughly secured to the barge, or that the load was balanced, or indeed positively buoyant. Ultimately she realised from their aggravated tones that, though the weight of the Duck was insufficient to swamp the barge, it was nonetheless pinning the vessel's underside against the ice-gravel shore. 'We're just going to have to run the motor hot,' said Cory. 'Otherwise it's not going to have enough motive force to move free of the shore. It should cope, it's immersed in a cooling medium.'

Junko evidently assented, but Portia thought she heard the other woman mutter 'Cock' as she ramped the engine.

The barge stayed afloat, but it was riding so low in the liquid that, even in the near-windless conditions, the lake's cryogenic methane washed across the deck at irregular intervals. Portia watched, unease rising in her like gorge. She didn't yet have control of the barge—that was in Junko's hands still, standing beside Cory on the shore with a portable control station—but once it was about two-thirds across, there would be handover to the cargo bay's station, and the fate of the barge, and the Duck, and perhaps the entire expedition would then rest on her fingertips and her judgment. It was a thought which unnerved her considerably more than did the plainly more hazardous prospect of diving to many metres' depth in the submersible which still waited its turn to travel on the barge.

The Duck's voyage across ran its course. She thought she'd been too slow to arrest the barge's motion, thought she had it misaligned for the landing stage, even thought for a few disastrous seconds that the barge was in fact riding too low to make it onto the landing stage; and what would they do then? She wiped hydrocarbon spray from her visor, swore as the gloves left a worse, more smeary mess in her field of view, swore again as the barge's underside groaned against the landing stage, and then it became apparent that things were more or less in place. She cut the power, breathed a sigh, then waited for the loud mechanical blows which would indicate that the barge was locked in.

She activated the elevator function, heard the plane's hydraulics complain at the load. But the barge was raised.

She untethered the Duck, prepared to climb aboard to drive it off the barge.

Well, that didn't go as badly as I thought. Perhaps things will work?

While the old Mitsuda Wavecutter didn't do anything fast, there was nothing truly hesitant, either, about the way in which it pushed itself skyward. Portia had watched from her webbing-wrapped seat at the back of the cockpit while Junko powered up the big craft's eight engines; it was clear to her that moments like these were what the slightly built pilot lived for. Across from Portia in his own tether of passenger webbing, Cory had seemed distinctly apprehensive as the flying boat's movement built steadily in speed and noise across Vänern's liquid-hydrocarbon expanse; but Portia knew the plane would lift in plenty of time, and indeed it did. Big plane, but bigger lake.

The Wavecutter's cruising speed, aloft, was marginally more than a hundred kilometres per hour, according to Junko; the flight would take between eleven and twelve hours. The first hour was spent in a steady and mostly smooth climb to an altitude of twenty-five kilometres, the ascent's few moments of turbulence never developing into anything truly troubling. The big plane's velocity was only slightly higher than that of an inter-settlement rail pod; though of course, this far north neither the terrain nor the population could support such a mode of transportation.

They were flying more-or-less due west; the flight would extend the night by three or four daycycles. Not that setting up in darkness was a problem, as Portia saw it; and at the depths to which she hoped to be diving, the ambient light level would be barely affected by whether it was daylight or night at the surface.

The plane levelled off. Junko invited them to unstrap themselves, if they wished, though she recommended they remain seated in case of turbulence. Cory fought his way out of confinement, stood up, crossed to a viewing port, stared out for several seconds, sat down again.

'We take passengers on some flights in summer,' Junko announced, as though it were the continuation of some earlier conversation. Perhaps it was. 'I mean, there's a passenger module, seating for forty-eight, which slots in at the front of the cargo bay. The winter years, it's strictly cargo, and significantly fewer flights, of course, because the population at Westlake and Zebker thins out in the absence of the tourist trade.'

'You think this bird has another summer in her?' Portia asked, the question emerging with more impertinence than she'd intended.

Junko, though, took it at face value, scanned from left to right across the cockpit before responding. 'One more, yeah, I reckon. Two I'd doubt.'

'Two and she'd be a museum piece,' said Portia.

'Hey, won't we all?' said Junko, and that was the end of the conversation for some time.

'Sleep, if you need to,' said Junko.

Portia turned to look at Cory. He did indeed look groggy, closed his eyes as if on command, sagged into the webbing.

Junko hadn't turned round from the controls once. How had she known that Cory, behind her, was starting to drift off?

With Cory drowsing, Portia thought, there was more of a prospect for dialogue with Junko, to clear the air on the past where that was needed. But it felt, also, like a duty to do so; in consequence, she doubted whether anything would be said. Junko was always one for keeping herself to herself: a quality which, somehow, seemed not a defect but an integral part of who she was. It was Junko's economy of language which ensured that when she did say something, one listened. She hadn't even complained about the change to the schedule necessitated, with Cory's accompaniment, by the need to load aboard the Duck and the trailer, and thereby to extend the loading process—and, she now realised, the unloading process, when they touched down on Kraken—by a couple of hours at each end. There had been a discussion, quite an animated one, with Cory on the mechanics of the process, but once that was settled, it was just a matter of tackling the task.

Portia both wanted and did not want to know what Junko made of Cory; but since she could not envisage any way of framing the question in a manner which didn't seem overly inquisitive, or needy, or both, she let it lie.

The engines' droning thrum, reassuringly regular, backgrounded her thoughts. There were still four, perhaps five, hours until Kraken was beneath them; currently, they must be flying parallel to, but south of, Ligeia. No settlements of any size on this route, no other air traffic, nothing to see when she looked out the viewing port, other than the plane's own running lights, marking out leading edge, engine nacelles, underwing floats. Save for the barely perceptible shifts in the plane's attitude as the air made itself felt against fuselage and wings—a motion which never rose to the level of turbulence—it was difficult not to believe that the craft was somehow at rest.

She must have slept, then, for a spell, because the descent had begun when she next became aware of herself.

The unloading went more smoothly. It helped that the anchorage was close in to shore, though to complicate matters the shoreline here, beyond the tidal drifts of sediment which would facilitate the submersible's launching, was deeply rutted with iceshingle-floored drainage channels and thus not suitable for an encampment; they would need to move the

Duck and the trailer to higher but more level ground approximately three hundred metres inland. It would make the preparations for each dive more cumbersome, but it could not be helped.

As before, they shipped across the trailer first. This time it was Cory who accompanied Junko on the first transit, and who would stay ashore to prepare for the Duck's arrival. There were a few helpless moments for Portia when it looked as though the barge had not grounded sufficiently for the trailer's unloading, but it passed without catastrophe.

The barge returned to the cargo hold. *Last chance to say something,* she told herself, but it was Junko who broke the silence, saying as her glovetips rested lightly on Portia's shoulder, 'I know that it must be painful, still, to talk about what happened. But if you need to, at any point, please reach out.'

There was an uncharacteristic gentleness to the pilot's tone; Portia found herself still unsure of how to respond. She did not want the dam to breach at this point. 'Thank you,' she said after what seemed like too long a pause, while she prepared to climb into the Duck to move it onto the barge. 'I guess it's no secret that I'm still struggling. I mean, I know why, but I still want to know why. If that makes sense. And I very much appreciate what you're doing for us.'

'It's the least I could do.'

'It's very much not, and you know it. I don't know how I would do this otherwise. So thank you.'

'You're— look, let's get this thing loaded. Your kid's waiting.'

'He's not my kid. He's my engineer-coder. Or my support crew. Or something. Apparently.'

'He seems chill enough, and capable. I hope it works out.'

And what did Junko mean by that?

She was right, though. It was time to load the Duck.

Junko flew off. They set up camp.

*

85

Though the first dive did not uncover any of the traces she sought, it went well, from a purely technical perspective. So too did the second, and the third.

The fourth did not.

It had become daylight, a long wan dawn. The walk down to the shore was through a broad gully, along which a thin methane stream unhurriedly made its way to the lowest level. With night having given way to a greyed sepia wash, highlit by a smear of sun indifferently illuminating the terrain's high points before them, the way seemed longer.

She was more conscious of the sound of Cory's breathing, rough, in her earpads than she was of her own. More conscious of his difficulties in maintaining a good footing, on the gully's iceshingle bed, than of hers; but then, she was more accustomed to fieldwork, her boot-treads better suited to unreliable terrain. Her mood was strange, unsettled; the sense was stronger, today, that this was destined to end in anticlimax than had been the case for the preceding three dives. A pattern had been set. It should have been an unsatisfying mindset, and in some senses it was, but it was also a sentiment to which she had been long accustomed through her research endeavours, and she knew that this was just something which needed to be pushed through. It might well not lead anywhere, but there was still a process; for her to follow the process was the only guarantee of ensuring that, though the day might be wasted, the time would not be. This was the thinking, the patience which Prof had sought to inculcate in her: a curious flavour of pessimistic optimism. In acting as she did, now, she was doing Prof's bidding. Was she doing her own?

She did not know, anymore. But the ache of the knowledge that Wiremu Garrity was not here to witness the endeavours that might yet bring a culmination to his efforts: that was a genuine physical pain, with a definite corporeal location across her forehead, across her chest, through her limbs.

They were on Bermoothes, a mostly craggy large island towards the southwest shore of Kraken's vast northern basin. Bermoothes, sufficiently isolated from the nearest population centres that it had never seen any settlement of its own, stretched roughly a hundred and twenty kilometres north to south, half that east to west at its widest. It was little more than a kinked range of rainworn hills embroidered with small seasonal lakes, its southeast rump forming the western shore of Kraken's throat, its south and southwest separated from the shore proper by the Hufaidh archipelago, a one-hundred-and-fifty-kilometre wide chaos of smaller islands—skerries, mostly—which made navigation to the mainland, in that direction, difficult by sea and impossible by land, even in a nominally amphibious vehicle such as the Duck. The northern half of Bermoothes—beyond the broad east-facing bay of Lulworth Sinus which almost bifurcated the isle—was surrounded by the wide open sea, and it was towards this which she had felt herself drawn for the past three years or more.

That was a change. The first time she'd been here, with Prof, it had been only the hope for the sonde's recovery which had steadied her; the setting's isolation, the sense of a vast separation from broader human companionship, was something which intimidated her. Now she could at least accept it—the landscape, the sense of emptiness—as something intrinsically without malice. It just was; there was nothing of menace here. Yet there might still be the prospect of discovery.

She stared out across the bay's slow-motion wave-ruffled surface, variegated by high cloud and weak sun. Her HUD aligned Lulworth's distant haze-dimmed headlands for her, between and beyond which Kraken awaited. The question of what was out there was sunk deep within her, her own molten core.

The submersible, blue banded with white, lay beached, awaiting. The thick multi-layered viewports which clustered towards its forward surface put her in mind of a jumping spider; the intakes and propulsion nozzles which framed it fore and aft, interrupting its otherwise smoothly curved hull, at least offered more directly aquatic associations. Nonetheless, it looked utterly out of place here on the shore of Titan's largest sea, for all that this was the very environment for which it had been designed and constructed. Not for the first time, she wondered what had led the Xu

87

family corporation to develop such a niche and probably unmarketable vehicle. *Gift horses*, she told herself, strove to adopt a more purposeful and focussed mindset. She worked with Cory to push it the few metres back towards the liquid, so he would be able to launch it unassisted once she had climbed aboard. She was sweating enough, by the time it was ready, that her suit had elected to release a fresh burst of scent to mask the odour of her exertion. As though she minded what the inside of her own suit smelled like.

They ran through the pre-launch checklist, each of them independently checking the hull for any sign of damage: all was ready. She signalled her own readiness, climbed atop to access and open the submersible's hatch. Prostrated herself within the narrow cavity of the airlock, face-forward; waited for the greenlighting on the status panel, shown within her HUD, which would confirm that the outer lock was closed, secured, and pressure-tight; felt her T-suit's slight stiffening as Titan's atmosphere was pumped out of the airlock; pressed the control for the inner hatch. Fell inelegantly through onto the pilot's couch: its padding was thick, doubling as insulation, intended as much to thermally distance the outer casing of the submersible's viewports from her body's waste heat as it was to safeguard her from Kraken's enveloping chill. She adjusted her posture into a semblance of comfort, checked what she could of the vessel's control display, jolted in sympathy to the craft's erratic lurches and slews as Cory's T-suit's servos laboured to push the submersible off the beach. At the back of her mind she felt that the current launch process was too primitive, too dependent on servo-boosted human exertion, potentially too abrasive; they should shape a slipway, or some similarly simple mechanism, rollers perhaps, to make the task easier and more routine. It was something which Cory could indeed work on, rather than simply waiting and worrying for her to resurface each time; but then it hardly seemed worth the effort, since they would be moving to a new site before too long. She had decided that they would spend one Titan day at the current site. She would run transects out from this site until her exploration of the bay, and of the local seafloor beyond it, had essentially been completed, and at the next dawn, fifteen daycycles hence, they would pack everything within the Duck and its trailer and would head north twenty kilometres or so, and start the exploration of a new strip of seafloor. In this way, within the three months or so that she expected their rations to last, they would be able to explore an expanse of seafloor approximately eighty by sixty kilometres: not a large fraction of the full size of Kraken, nor even of that fraction of Kraken which lay north of the throat, but her expectation was that what she sought was most likely to be found within that zone. And if she found nothing, the details of the region's submarine topography, mapped at comparatively high resolution, would still hold some value. There had been talk, for example, of setting up a tidally driven ethane refinery just north of the throat, either on Bermoothes' east coast or on the shore of the mainland opposite, though it had come to nothing as yet.

The submersible's attitude shifted again, less abruptly: now it floated free in the chalky liquid of the shoreline. She could hear through her helmet's earpieces, vague and distorted, the staticky slosh which marked Cory's trudged retreat, from knee-depth, out of the numbingly cold liquid. She smirked as he swore, as was becoming a habit, in complaint against the submersible's mass and obduracy. Yes, maybe they should work on a slipway or something.

But that was a thought for later, really. Now to persuade the vessel to sink.

Central to the submersible's operation were four chambers that ran, just beneath its C-fibre skin, for most of the vessel's length, an upper and a lower chamber on each side, and each by volume almost the equal of the cramped cockpit around which they were arrayed like the four rods of a quadrupole mass filter. Currently the methane/ethane/nitrogen mix within these chambers was vaporised, providing buoyancy. Portia bled the gas from the lower chambers and activated the intake valves, drawing Kraken's chill liquid into the lower tanks and causing the submersible to settle gradually lower. When this had proceeded sufficiently, she repeated the process with the upper chambers. Even through the multiple layers of insulation cocooning the cockpit within the submersible's outer hull, even through the additional insulation of her T-suit, she fancied that she could feel the cold pressing in on her from both sides, though the cabin temperature readout did not support this conjecture. When the readings on her HUD told her the tanks were sufficiently full for ballast purposes, when the submersible could function as its descriptor stated, she prepped the propulsion system.

Kraken provided the ballast; Kraken provided the buoyancy; Kraken provided the propulsion. Liquid from the ballast tanks was drawn into smaller chambers at the rear, heated to a moderate degree under confinement, then the resultant pressurised gas was ejected to provide thrust. There were aspects to this mechanism which were not ideal: it became less effective and more power-hungry as a function of increasing depth, which ultimately placed a floor of approximately one hundred and twenty metres on the submersible's operation, below which the vessel could not safely descend. Much of Kraken's seafloor was within this limit, but there were also trenches, out past the heads, which ran much deeper. She'd have to hope that what she sought was not beyond reach.

She activated the propulsors, under the lowest power setting to begin with. This allowed her to complete the necessary final set of pre-dive checks while the craft was still close enough to shore that the dive could be aborted without risk. Power, heat exchange, life support and telemetry were all problem-free. Attitude control was acceptable, though the vessel's forward motion was always slightly shaky, as though it were constantly fighting its way through turbulence. She had stopped worrying about it; probably it was just a characteristic relating to the craft's small size, or due to stochastic fluctuations in its approximation to neutral buoyancy. Certainly its performance hadn't deteriorated, in that regard, since the first dive three sleeps ago.

Anyway, the submersible was ready. Time to venture.

She would not be within radio contact of Cory once she was submerged; there had been talk of rigging together an acoustic generator to allow at least minimal signalling from the depths, but with all the other late-stage modifications required, there hadn't been time for that.

She'd be on her own, each time. It didn't overly concern her; the submersible had proven itself reliable.

She took it out and down. This close to shore, the depth was only a dozen metres, and some diffuse lighting permeated to the floor of the bay, casting a webwork of vague shadow which was difficult to discern in the headlights' glare but which, when she had cracked her helmet's seal and had removed her helmet (and her gloves), was subliminally evident in her peripheral vision as shapes which slowly moved back past the submersible's sides. It was an eerie vista, lumpen and pocked, all contours softened by the sedimentation of infalling haze particles across the millennia, minimally reshaped by the regular but slight tidal movement within the bay.

She wrinkled her nose. There were some who claimed to be able to distinguish between the tholin deposits of different regions of Titan on the basis of odour, with the haze produced by polar photochemical processes in the northern or southern summer having a distinctive character—stronger, sharper, somehow deader—that was not evident in the atmospheric detritus of the temperate or equatorial regions. While she didn't directly subscribe to this view herself, it was undeniable that something she had stepped in—whether on the walk down to the shore or in the Kraken shallows while she was preparing to board—stank of decomposing bleach and burnt metal. She briefly considered replacing her helmet, but chose instead to ride out the smell. The helmet, with its generally informative HUD, carried disadvantages of its own: the HUD could only make sense of what it could recognise and interpret. The visor made it that much harder for her eyes to discern for themselves, through the submersible's viewports, the kind of details for which she was searching.

Not that she had any real understanding of what those details were. There was just the conviction that, if she saw them, she would know. An irregularity, a foreignness, a not-belonging. Something like the submersible itself, in other words. Or like her.

The submersible's hull thrummed, the cockpit stank, its air and control panels were almost painfully cold. She liked it that way: cold diving was clear-headed diving.

She was moving beyond hope of any intervention, at a forward velocity of around ten kilometres per hour and a rate of descent, currently, of approximately half a metre per minute. At its current speed, it would take almost three hours to clear the Lulworth Heads and to reach the open sea. While that step had been a feature of each dive she'd done here, she wasn't simply retracing her path from the days before: each dive, she took a new arc through the bay, and a different route on the return. The sub's instruments performed detailed mapping of the submerged and sediment-coated terrain beneath the vessel and monitored temperature, density, and composition gradients within the liquid's methane–ethane–nitrogen blend, while she grimaced against the chill and gazed out to see what, if anything, lay ahead. She was happy.

The submersible was not. Forty minutes in, the lower left propulsor failed, subtly changing the soundscape within the cabin and threatening to slew the vessel. Portia cut the heating to the upper right propulsor to compensate while she toggled various settings to scry out the issue with the stalled unit. With fewer drive units operating, the motion was both more erratic and slower. It couldn't be helped. With luck, it would just be a matter of resting and rebooting the glitched propulsor.

Two minutes later, the lower right unit stalled also.

Fuck.

It was the lower propulsors which were capable of providing lift thrust as well as forward momentum; though the upper propulsors could facilitate descent, or could be operated for direct forward thrust, they couldn't be used to propel the neutrally buoyed craft to the surface. It was still possible to use the principle of buoyancy to ensure surfacing, but this necessitated heating and bleeding the tanked methane after closing the intake valves. Since it wasn't currently possible to purge the lower tanks, she would have to bleed the upper methane chambers. But with the submersible buoyed to the surface, it wouldn't then be possible to draw in sea-liquid through the upper intakes.

She could press ahead, could use the upper propulsors to descend and to move forward at reduced speed, to carry on the mapping mission and the search while she waited for whatever had glitched to right itself.

But there were stupid risks inherent in that idea; it was safest to retreat, to limp somehow back to base and to figure out, with Cory's assistance and devil's advocacy, what had gone wrong and then to rectify it. They would lose perhaps one or two or three days but nothing more. She was reaching for the controls to turn the submersible about when there was a muffled explosion behind her. The vessel yawed. She cut all heat to the units, waiting for the craft's attitude to settle so she could evaluate her best next move; all the time waiting, too, for an intensification of the cold or the odour of Titan, for some signal of the hull breach which would doom her. It didn't come.

She would have to turn the vessel about and then to make slowly back to shore. Ordinarily, on the grounds both of safety and of optimal propulsor performance, it was best to run close to the surface, only barely submerged. But the upper propulsors would need to vent most of their methane reserves in order to generate sufficient buoyancy to bring her close to the surface; and if she breached, if she effectively overshot the ascent, it might well leave the upper tank inlets unable to take in the liquid required for subsequent propulsion. She would be becalmed, or close to it, five or six kilometres from shore and with no way to return that did not popsicle her. Best, therefore, to continue to operate where it was clear that the upper propulsors would still work to push the craft forward: thus, at depth.

She put her helmet back on; kept the gloves off, for now, for ease of operation of the controls. The helmet provided one layer more of possibly illusory protection. Plus it was more straightforward to group the metrics she needed in the HUD, by verbal command to the suit's intellect, than to try to persuade the submersible itself to show her what she needed; designed for routine operation, its display did not lend itself to the requirements of troubleshooting. There hadn't been time to finesse that.

She fed heat to the upper right drive chamber to create the slow burp of thrust needed to steer the craft around. The vessel cooperated, but it was canting as it did so, banking more than was required: there must be a serious misdistribution of mass across the tanks. Indeed, she was seeing, with the HUD's assistance, that the lower left chamber was almost entirely full of liquid. It had not been five minutes ago, and it had been sealed throughout that time at both the inlet and propulsor ends.

There was a leak. Kraken had found its way in.

She must not give in to panic. All thirty years of her life on Titan, and a decade of fieldwork, had taught her to measure the danger posed by the environment, to not exaggerate that danger, to respond as needed to maximise the odds on survival. First it was necessary to check everything: rapidly, to identify immediate hazards and threats to life, then more methodically to ensure no mistakes were made. There was still no odour or extreme chill indicating a cockpit breach, nor were the craft's controls compromised except for those relating to the lower left methane chamber and its drive system. Were there a fissure within the outer hull anywhere, she very likely would not still have that level of control. So, in all probability, the leak was only into the lower left chamber, was still isolated from the broader spaces within the hull. It was bad, but it was not—or not necessarily—a death blow. She could still compensate for the craft's infirmities, could still persuade the damaged vessel to crawl to shore. It would require careful, responsive adjustment of the upper propulsors' vectors of thrust to do so. Now, she needed—

A wall appeared in the immediate foreground, a steep and in places almost ghost-pale face of weathered ice directly in her path. Fifty metres ahead; forty; thirty-five. The ridge's upper rim was only three or four metres above the submersible's path, and still at a depth of twenty metres or more. She needed to climb; but with the lower propulsors inactivated, she could not, and there was no clearance to dive, either. She threw heat at the upper right propulsor to sharpen the turn; but the change in heading was not sufficient. Twenty-five; fifteen; ten. Still turning, still canting, but not enough. Five. She braced for impact.

It happened as in slow motion. A thump, ominous and intense, on the forward edge of the craft's underside. The blow, sufficient to throw her from the pilot's couch, knocked her helmet-first against an auxiliary viewport's upper edge with a sickening crack. The vessel skewed, a secondary impact thudded against the underside's rear, then all sense of balance was lost: she was on her side against the cockpit wall, the craft still twisting around some indefinable axis. Then the collision was done. Blood in her mouth, an ache where she'd landed against her arm. She'd pissed herself. Not that the suit wasn't prepared for that eventuality, on a twelve-hour dive.

She took stock, sprawled on a surface which had never been designed to comfortably support a T-suited human. There was one major, obvious problem, but by itself it wasn't what would kill her. Of the things which might be lethal: her instruments were blind, outward vision lost. The collision had stirred up aeons' worth of the fine sedimentary deposits of tholin and other detritus which covered every submerged surface. The craft would separate, in time, from the churned clouds of sediment, but she would need to bring the scanning and nav systems back online, or she was doomed.

At least she'd have some time to do so: the submersible's hull apparently remained intact. The fracture which had occurred in the initial impact was in her helmet's visor, not the viewport. Though this was ultimately almost as bad.

Assuming she made it to the surface, assuming she made it back to the shore, exiting the craft with a breached helmet would be a quick death in the vessel's current configuration.

Somehow, the submersible had found Stable Two. It was drifting upside down, the cold of the airlock's inner hatch pressed beneath her suit's front.

Well, fuck.

seven

Wind-scraped, barren, fringed by dark damp sand: the beach which marked the central curve of Lulworth Sinus managed to make something dismal of even the rising winter sun, visible only as an uncertain blur of pale grey between east and southeast. Out past the bay's headlands, in the channel which broadened north of Seldon Fretum—otherwise known as Kraken's throat—the tidal current might well be raising slow-crashing wavetops; here in the bay, there was little more than a silty wash which played at the sides of Cory's boots, fizzing slightly from the faint aura of waste heat leaking from his suit. He stood for a time at the liquid's edge, in the shallow indentation which the submersible's launching had carved into its saturated sediment. Though that event had gone as well as the three earlier forays here, Cory could not do otherwise than worry, and there was, in truth, not much else he could do at the moment. When the submersible returned there would be the need for systems to be checked, and for the performance of all of the craft's critical mechanisms to be assessed against wear, degradation, and the prospect of failure. Right now, while the submersible was out at depth and far from his reach, the most expeditious use of his time might be to seek to rest, to sleep, so as to be refreshed and ready for activity later; but this wasn't possible for him. It was natural, he supposed, to have an apprehension born of the sense of responsibility which he carried for the vessel's safe operation.

Was it the craft for which he was concerned—worried—or was it its occupant's safety? It was not as easy to answer that question as he felt it should be. The two were connected, of course, but that didn't fully explain the difficulty.

It was in his nature to worry, more than he thought it was in other people's. Although perhaps it was simply that other people hid it; as did he, of course, though he always felt that the charade was, on his part, something by which those around him were not fooled. Certainly it was a characteristic of his of which Arum had always been well aware, and one which, now that he dwelt upon it, she had sometimes used to her advantage. It seemed, now (as he wondered why it had not so seemed previously) that he had made—to himself, and to others—many excuses for Arum, and for Arum's conduct, over the years during which he and she had had some form of relationship: Arum chose not to meet others of his acquaintance, because Arum was private; Arum did not need to explain her occasional unexpected or unforeshadowed disappearances, because Arum was independent; Arum never spoke of the others with whom she had occasion or need to interact, because Arum did not wish to betray confidences. All of these were markers placed down upon the landscape of their shared experience, delimiting that landscape, and glowing in visibility blue; and he had chosen to ignore them, to minimise them as signals of any concern. The truth was that Arum's ways were not in themselves problematic, had this conduct and this sense of expectation been mutual; but, as he could now see, she had actively worked to persuade him to tell her, in detail, what he had been up to, while she had been absent, and what those around him (whom she did not wish to meet) had done and thought and intended and planned. There'd been an inquisitiveness to her, alongside the evasiveness; he'd seen it, but hadn't dared to challenge it.

He had trusted her throughout because he had wanted to be trusted by her; it was as simple as that, and as misguided. He still wished her no harm, but there was nothing left beyond that. Nothing, save this occasional tendency to dwell on that portion of the past; perhaps to seek to learn from it.

Had he learnt from it? Was his trust, now, of Portia similarly misguided? Arum had lied to him; Portia had lied to him; but it seemed that the root cause of Portia's efforts at deception had been different, resulting from a fear for safety rather than from—say it!—a desire to manipulate. And Portia had never lied about the most important thing she had told him, which had been Teresa Maria's death. He did not trust Portia absolutely, as he had once placed complete trust in Arum, but he felt, now, that Portia was more deserving than was his former lover. In part, this was why he was still here.

Of course, it was the nature of human interaction that the verity of this view would be properly established only through hindsight. Life, by necessity, made historians of everyone. It made liars of most, too; he'd lied to Arum, himself. Ligeia, when he'd known it was Kraken. He still didn't know, completely, why he'd done that, didn't know if she believed the lie; it would be entirely in keeping with his current understanding of her nature that she would not let on that she had caught him out.

Might she know, now, where he and Portia were? Might she have shared that information with her former (and perhaps still current) associates? There wasn't any way to tell, any more than there was any way to establish whether his helmet was genuinely free of the patchware with which she'd loaded it. He'd checked it, to the utmost of his abilities, over the past few days, and it had seemed uncontaminated, but he lacked the aptitude, the expertise, the proprietary knowledge required to crack the base-level operating code of a commercial T-suit helmet, and so he could not be sure.

He suspected that Arum also still lacked that ability, which meant she had likely had help. That didn't necessarily make a lie of her latest assertion—that she was seeking to complete her disassociation from the pharmhands, and required plausible detail on Portia's and Cory's activities to effect that goal—but it did mean he would need to plan for the possibility that she might know where he was, and that others might also know as a consequence. He was, still, a fugitive, both from the pol and from those opposed to the pol, because of what had happened on that long night more than a year ago.

If the pol knew where he was, they would be here already; they had no reason to delay. The pol were not here, therefore they didn't know the combination of his whereabouts and his identity. But the pharmhands would have reason to delay. Ambush and robbery were stock-in-trade to them, and Cory and Portia didn't yet have anything worth taking.

They would *still* not have anything worth taking, even if Portia's search succeeded; but the pharmhands didn't know this. Assuming the bandits' goal was plunder rather than simple revenge, they would not move in too soon.

It was useless for Cory to wait at the beach. She would be out for several hours; he may as well get back to the encampment and clear out the Duck's latrine-waste tank.

Making his way up the ice-gravelled streambed which was the most direct route back to their encampment, Cory reflected on what had passed between the two of them on the previous daycycle, at the conclusion of Portia's third dive into Kraken's depths. She'd been in an ebullient mood, buoyant, much more so than after her earlier dives. She had watched him with animated impatience while he performed his post-dive diagnostics on the submersible; she'd moved hurriedly up the gully, not watching her footing in her haste, slipping two or three times on the way; she'd been visibly distracted all through the shared silence of the daycycle's last meal. It had been evident that something was stirring within her; Cory had thought better than to push for any kind of explanation. Had she found something? Perhaps so. If she wished to, she'd speak her mind.

She'd stood up, seemingly on the pretext of collecting the remnants of her meal and his, and of transferring them to the cycler. Those tasks completed, she had crossed the prefab's floor to her personal effects locker, had removed something, had returned to her bench, an imperfectly suppressed grin upon her face. 'Here,' she'd called out, and she'd thrown something, in a leisurely toss, towards him. He'd caught it. A slab of plastic. An irregular chunk of something which had been planar, or nearly so, roughly four centimetres thick and perhaps twenty centimetres across its longest axis, fifteen perpendicular to that. Undifferentiated grey polymer, unexpected involutions along its edges at odds with the more-or-less smooth flat faces.

He'd seen her remove it from the locker. 'You didn't find this today.' (Nor the previous two days, obviously. It didn't smell like something which had been in Kraken. It didn't smell like anything which had been outside much at all.)

'No,' she'd replied. 'I didn't find anything today.'

He'd inspected it, weighed it in his hand. 'What is it?' he'd asked.

'It's why we're here.'

'It looks printed. And it's hollow.'

'Both of those things, yes. Wiremu had it printed. It's one of three copies he had made.'

'Copies?'

'It's a replica. Of something we found when Wiremu and I returned to Kraken three years ago, when we went to find and retrieve the sonde, our submersible instrumentation package, which had been lost when Junko's ekranoplan made an emergency splashdown. We found two chunks of that type, connected by short stems to a length of composite-polymer cable which had somehow snared the sonde as it trailed behind us during flight. The objects, the original objects of which this is a copy, are polymer too, but a much more complicated composite than anything routinely used. This was the larger of the two specimens. And what you hold in your hand is new, only a couple of years old, but what we found was considerably older.'

'What is it?' he'd repeated.

'We don't know. The print is a match for the overall density and the mass distribution of the original, so yes, it was also hollow. It might have been part of a buoyancy aid, given it was found in Kraken's shallows, or its purpose could be completely unrelated to immersion. We had no way of knowing. But it's old, and we think it's from very far away.'

'It looks decidedly unprepossessing,' he'd said. 'How can you be in any way sure of its origins?'

'We can't,' she'd responded, then her voice had picked up with something which he guessed was suppressed excitement. 'But four things. Firstly, the polymer composite. Carbon fourteen content zero, which doesn't prove great age, but it's at least suggestive. It implies, at least, that this was not constructed anywhere with a nitrogen-containing atmosphere within the historical era, or if it was then extreme expense must have been spent to rid it of any C-14 content. But why? That's also true, by the way, of the tholin sediment traces on its casing, and who would go to the effort and cost of synthesising C-14-depleted tholin? Then there were the contents.'

'You said it was hollow.'

'Yes. Or more accurately pocketed, like an armoured foam material. The outermost pockets, those nearest the edges, had been contaminated by Kraken, but the central portion contained gas.'

'That's it?'

'We had it analysed. The confined gas was a mixture of noble gases. Inert gases. Helium, neon, argon, krypton. That's the other three things. Much more helium than anything else, but much more neon than argon. That's the second thing. Third, the helium was almost forty percent helium three, and four, the argon was almost exclusively argon thirty-six, with about five percent of thirty-eight and negligible argon forty.'

'I'm sorry, you've lost me.'

'Those are not standard terrestrial abundances. That is, they don't correspond in any respect to the usual rocky-world abundances of the inert gases. On Earth, on Titan, anywhere with a solid surface, almost all the helium you find will be helium four, and the argon will be argon forty, from radiological processes. This chunk, that is the original, is— was depleted in those, compared to the other isotopes, and the neon abundance was off-the-scale high in comparison, almost protosolar. So based on the gas mixture it contained, this object wasn't constructed anywhere that people live; the abundances don't match the giant planets either; and it appears to be extremely old. So you tell me. It's undeniably constructed, but if people didn't construct it...'

He'd stared at the misshapen object in his hand. With a little imagination, it could be part of an outsized egg casing. 'What makes you so sure it was constructed? It looks almost organic. I mean, of biological origin. Like a slab of something like bird-bone.'

'We considered that, at the start. But what kind of biological process results in sequestering only noble gases, out of everything else?'

'And this is what you've been keeping secret? From everyone?' He'd looked up. 'Does the pilot know? Junku?'

'Junko. She was there, so she knows parts, obviously. Not the whole, and she's not curious. She's Wiremu's sister-in-law, ex-sister-in-law now, I suppose, I always felt she thought she'd maybe chosen the wrong brother. I trust her, because Prof trusted her. And the analytical labs where we had the gas and the polymer characterised, they must know parts too. But Wiremu was careful to approach them with a plausible cover story. They get a lot of odd requests from geochem surveys and the like; I doubt they'd have pieced together anything approaching the true nature of what they were working with in this instance.'

'Which is?'

She'd rolled her eyes. 'Who knows? Prof had plenty of theories, it seemed like a new one every week. But what we had, it was both too much and too little to explain. That's why we were going to search for more, to try to find what this was part of. To get something publishable.'

'Publishable?'

'It's academia, Cory. That's what's important. And this… it's intriguing, but it's not enough.'

'So you think there's more of whatever this is? Something this came from, presumably submerged? In Kraken?'

'Who knows?' she'd said again. 'But the length of cable that chunk had been attached to, when we found the sonde… it wasn't enough to have brought down the sonde by its own weight. Nowhere near. It must have been tethered to something larger, something which it broke free of, itself, in its collision with the sonde.'

'How much larger?'

'The sonde line was monofilament. They're not designed to break, and it didn't. The anchorage point on the ekranoplan's underside, that was what gave out. So I'm thinking several thousand kilograms, as a lower limit.'

'Several tonnes?'

'As a lower limit. And before you ask, yes, we went looking for it, to the extent we were able. Didn't find a trace. But it has to be down there.'

He'd not slept well, after that.

At the bend in the streambed, where the course wrapped its way around a large ice boulder which was evidently more resistant to erosion than the surrounding landscape had been, Cory thought he heard something. A muffled slap, an object of moderate size falling from a low height. Something of that nature. Though he'd heard it through the helmet's earpads, it wasn't something which had come through on comms; it was something his suit's external microphones had picked up against the swathed quiet surrounding his own exertions. His natural instinct was to turn to the shore at the foot of the gentle slope behind him, where he could expect to see the submersible's headlamps when Portia brought it in. But that would be hours still, and the suit didn't think the sound had come from there. It had originated, approximately, in the direction of the encampment.

Cory grew concerned, picked up the pace, scrabbled up the steepest section of the gravel-choked rapids. Slipped. Swore, caught himself, amped up the suit's inbound audio until the static drowned out his tinnitus. There was no repeat of the sound he'd heard, the blow or the fall, whatever it had been. But after two more minutes, when he was no more than thirty seconds from the ridge that lay between him and the encampment, there was a rolling burst of noise from that direction: the rumble of a vehicle motor, revved loud, almost aggressively performative. A skid-bike or a two-person half-track, he thought, going by the sound. Not the Duck, at any rate. He stopped. Was contemplating the best next move when the noise of the explosion flared in his helmet. The explosion, too, had come from the direction of the encampment. When his hearing had recovered some seconds later, the vehicle noise had abated.

Something shifted in the landscape beyond the ridge. Something which became aerial: a motorised glider, its harness bearing a T-suited figure. The glider was heading in the general direction of Hufaidh, and beyond that the mainland.

From the direction of the encampment, also, a plume of dark smoke.

Reaching the Duck—which itself appeared to be intact—he could see that the prefab outbuilding would be of no further use to them. The smoke was already dissipating: Titan didn't tolerate combustion. But the explosion had sheared off the rigid outer hatch of the secondary airlock, fragments of which had been flung almost as far as the Duck's front windscreen, twenty metres away. The blast had evidently also ruptured the outbuilding's inner lock: as he watched, a numbing helplessness gripping him, the structure slumped in on itself in a slow collapse, its argonogel-reinforced walls splaying and canting as Titan found its way into the realm from which it had previously been denied, turning it as lethal as the rest of the moon.

Approaching, he confirmed that the Duck remained unscathed by the blast's shrapnel. The trailer, the already overdue rental trailer, hadn't fared so well, though it clearly hadn't been the attack's main target.

A kind of grief took hold of him, stayed with him while the voice in his helmet told him: 'Don't try to deceive us again. When you've found what you seek, we'll be back. In force. Cooperate, and you'll live.'

A Coustenis accent, slow drawn-out vowels, low in timbre. Male. A voice with no warmth in it, no audible doubt either. An arrogant tone, accustomed to getting its way.

Laith. He'd never heard the other speak, but he was sure of it. Something chilled inside him.

He surveyed the wreckage briefly, then turned to make his way back down to the shore. What else could he do?

eight

Kraken was ancient; Kraken was vast; Kraken was cold far beyond the limits of historical human experience. Kraken was both mythologised and feared, more so than any other place on Titan; and yet by some measures, its reputation was as outsized as was itself. Far more people had died, through misadventure, technical failure or simple ill luck, along the shores of Titan's multitudinous smaller bodies of ultracold liquid hydrocarbon; more too had fallen, beyond the prospect of rescue, at times even of retrieval, into the depths of those smaller seas and lakes. Regardless, Kraken's reputation could not be dispelled. Planes had been lost within it, boats had disappeared into its depths. There were, on Titan, something like one hundred and fifty grave markers for which the location of the relevant human remains was not much more precisely known than 'somewhere in Kraken', with every year one or two or five more names added to that list. Her own had nearly become one of those, five years ago.

Kraken didn't care whether it caused one's death; but it was not in the habit of giving second chances.

nine

It was too soon for him to admit genuine concern regarding Portia's whereabouts—the dive would take as long as it took, and she was not nominally due back for another two hours—but Cory was worried nonetheless. He couldn't clearly separate the personal threat posed by Laith and associates from the utterly impersonal threat of Kraken's extreme environment: in his mind, in the aftermath of the outbuilding's bombing, the one led to the other and back again. Not twenty-four hours ago, Portia had finally explained for him some of the motivation which drove her, within the structure that had become their makeshift home at the site. Now that structure was uninhabitable, irreparable.

The shore was still. A low smudge of sun towards the right-hand edge of his vision, the stripe of its pale and diffused reflection on the otherwise-dark liquid, the sandy silty sediment. The sound of breathing. The languid, backgrounded trickle of the methane stream. The sense of a lapse, before something grim would befall him and Portia.

It seemed likely, he thought, that the pharmhands—now personified by Laith—would give them some time, in the event that he and Portia did not inadvertently signal to them that the search had succeeded. He was confident that such signalling could be avoided; it was merely a matter of ensuring that they did not communicate anything of sensitivity while suited. They would have daycycles, certainly, possibly weeks to continue to search for whatever secret Kraken held. Laith would know that they could not both escape in a one-person submersible; would know also that there was no overland route back to civilisation. If he and Portia stayed together, then they were both pinned down here on Bermoothes; though they could call for help, it would take time to arrive, time which likely would not be afforded them.

Ultimately, the pharmhands' patience would be exhausted, when they considered that too much time had elapsed, or that some limit had been crossed: they would move in. And this time they would not merely restrict the destruction to property. If they were not accorded what they considered was theirs to take, they'd get what they wanted by right of force.

Cory had seen off pharmhands before, but that had been with gear he no longer had, with allies who had departed him. And maybe, in a sense, that was the problem.

His aunt had accompanied Wiremu and Portia; now he was accompanying Portia. Both of those must have been affronts to the pharmhands around Ponnamperuna and Neimann; and who knew how loyalties were traded among the rival gangs? It had perhaps been Teresa Maria's involvement with Wiremu and his colleague which had drawn their attention, had possibly even bolstered a sense of need for revenge, and the same could be exactly true also of his work at Portia's side.

And it had been his own allegiance to Arum, rather than to the aunt to whom he owed his life, which had been a factor in Teresa Maria's decision to—

It was useless to speculate. What was needed was to plan, if he could only see how to do that. To plan, and to prepare, and to wait. Then to act.

The sun had moved, the cloud cover had increased, and Portia hadn't returned. Cory's unease had taken on some solidity. The previous dives had not taken this long. Either she had found something, or she had struck trouble. Neither was good, on a day when Laith had as much as promised to return at the first indication of the mission's success.

Never mind that what Portia sought was of no value whatsoever to Laith. Cory would need to warn her, in private, not to communicate anything of sensitive substance via the suit; and he could not safely do so while they were still suited.

For now, of course, the point was academic. There was no communication.

He had returned to the encampment. He'd tasked himself with retrieving anything useful which could be collected from the wrecked outbuilding. First he'd flensed it: an activity which felt morally wrong, vandalistic. It wasn't his property, after all. But the structure was irreparable anyway, and it would have been needlessly hazardous to attempt to rummage within its collapsed sheath. Peeled apart, its contents were revealed in disarray, and with significant damage to many items. Worst affected were the tools and instruments which had been housed within the structure's workroom, close to the blast's locus. More than half of the workroom's gear was now unusable, broken or distorted or no longer reliable. That was a major concern: if the submersible required maintenance or repair, would he still have the necessary equipment?

First priority, though, were the foodstuffs. Aside from two or three which had fallen out and spilled their now congealed contents, the rack of ready-prepareds was mostly undamaged, though thoroughly frozen through. He hefted the rack around to the Duck's secondary airlock, stowed it within and set the lock on a repeated purge-and-filter cycle to allow the wrappers to outgas so they didn't carry the offputting aroma of Titan.

Clothing and personal effects. Not much of his—he believed in travelling light (and at any rate hadn't packed for an extended campaign)—but Portia had rather more. It didn't feel right to sort through it in her absence; he simply bagged it, hurriedly, not caring to catalogue it as he went, and placed it in the Duck's cab airlock. Then the power units, and whatever in the wrecked workroom was still usable. Last there was the flooring, much of which was undamaged. He stacked it back in the trailer.

He belatedly remembered the nav-drone, nestled in its Duck-top cradle.

Torn between the sense of urgency associated with searching for signs of the submersible, and with the suddenly pressing need for food, he forced himself to gulp down just enough of a snack-strip to dull the worst of his hunger before taking the drone down to the still-deserted beach.

He flew it out as far as he dared; it saw nothing.

He didn't sleep well at the end of that daycycle. It was clear now that something had gone wrong.

Though the movement of the Sun across the sky was largely lateral this far north at this point in the long Saturnian year, it was nonetheless also noticeably higher today.

There was still nothing to see from his vantage point; just sea-liquid, shoreline, cloud cover, haze. He sent the drone up, commanding it again through his helmet's HUD.

It occurred to him, belatedly, that this might allow Laith and others to monitor the drone's flights also, through the intercept which Arum had inserted in his helmet's ware. But he could not be bothered worrying about that now. It was more important to try to find out what had happened to Portia.

The drone had a nominal return range of five kilometres on full charge, but he was loath to send it out anywhere near that distance. His helmet's transmitter was sufficient to directly control it out to, at most, barely one kilometre. And though it could be pre-programmed to return from a further distance, there were risks in doing so. If he overtaxed it he might lose it, and it was currently his best hope of finding Portia's submersible.

He sent it out five hundred metres due east, radar-mapping the sea surface as he went, saw nothing, brought it quickly back to shore. Swapped out the power unit, sent it out again, east-south-east, nothing; ranged across to south-south-east, beckoned it back. Saw something almost three hundred metres distant. Hovered. Descended for a closer inspection and for visual confirmation. His HUD showed a solid surface, pale, inundated, lying canted with one edge just proud of the surrounding liquid. The drone's analytics indicated a commercial C-fibre composition, a visibility-blue sheath lightly scored by abrasive action.

He'd found the submersible.

His relief was rapidly tempered by two details: the craft wasn't moving, wasn't even discernibly drifting, and it was capsized.

ten

He brought the drone back, not directly to him but perpendicular to the submersible stranded offshore. Then he walked to retrieve the drone.

Now that he knew where to look, and with the visual augmentations made possible by the HUD, he could see the submersible himself, just barely. The bay curved around to meet it, to some extent, but it remained disturbingly distant from the shore; there was no hope in that separation.

The shore here was craggier, an expanse of tholin-stained ice worn somewhat smooth but nonetheless still predominantly lumpy, lacking the upper stratum of sandy sediment which had been swept onto the beach by tidal activity or the occasional rain-fed flooding of the stream gully those few hundred metres north. The gulf between him and the submersible, around one hundred and forty metres in a straight line, was too great for a T-suit to traverse before its occupant succumbed to hypothermia. He couldn't reach it; and even if Portia were still capable of exiting the craft, even if there was a way in which to do that while it lay stranded, airlock down, on what seemed to be a sandbar, she couldn't make the shore. There was nothing—

That wasn't correct, though. There was a lakesuit. It was Portia's, but it might still fit him.

The suit didn't fit well—Portia was a few centimetres taller, and more slender—but it would seal, he thought, and movement would be possible.

Nonetheless, it was odd wearing another's suit; wearing a woman's suit; wearing Portia's lakesuit. The plumbing was different. He'd just have to hope that he would need the suit for a short enough interval that this wouldn't be a problem.

The immediate problem was that it didn't recognise him.

'Suit system access, please. Life support, comms, servos, thermal management.'

<Please identify yourself.>

'I don't have time. I'm her contractor, I need access. Portia is in difficulties, in Kraken, and requires rescue. System access, please.'

<You are still required to identify yourself.>

'I'm her contractor.'

<I still require your name.>

'Cory. Cory Krishnamurthy. Can we please just—'

<Access granted. Have you operated a lakesuit previously?>

'No, but— Can we do this another time?'

<We can, but there are some basic features of operation which you'll need to be across.>

'Can we at least run through those while I walk to the shore?'

<Undivided attention is preferable.>

'So is a successful rescue. Transfer motion control, please.'

<Motion control transferred.>

Servo operation in the lakesuit required a lighter touch than in a standard T-suit, which was counterintuitive given the lakesuit's substantially greater bulk. This was indeed one of the first points covered in the suit's initial-use tutorial, but Cory was already well aware of the phenomenon by then. He had resorted to a kind of shuffle to ensure he did not stumble repeatedly, in the ill-fitting and overpowered suit, as he managed the steeper sections of the stream leading down to the shore.

Actually, it made sense. The suit was designed for movement through liquid; the servos were calibrated to make this feel natural.

He reached the shore, moved down to where he had left the drone as a location marker. Gazed out at the sea. The suit's HUD was unfamiliar, differently configured, and it took him several seconds to be sure he was seeing the capsized submersible.

'How do I navigate to that object? The submersible?' he asked the suit. 'By vision?'

<A false-colour overlay can be provided,> replied the suit. *<But vision in sea liquid is intrinsically unreliable, as sediment is typically stirred up in operation. This suit is equipped with inertial reckoning, which for your purposes is likely more suitable. Do you wish to deploy?>*

'Yes.'

<Please state reference targets.>

'The submersible. And back here.'

<Configured.>

He'd have around thirty minutes' full immersion, he knew, before thermoregulation became unreliable. That should be comfortably enough to reach the submersible, and to return to shore, but it wasn't a lot of time to achieve anything more; it was certainly not sufficient for a rescue. But understanding, in detail, the task which he faced was the first step in formulating a process by which to retrieve the submersible, or at least to manoeuvre it to a point sufficiently close to the shore that it was safe for Portia to disembark.

Of course, it would also be good to think of a way by which to right the submersible, so as to provide access to its airlock. But first steps first.

He strode into Kraken, feeling carefully for his balance. The liquid effervesced around his suit's legs as waste heat escaped from the servoes. The sedimented uneven terrain beneath him was instantly a challenge, as was the sense of profound cold. Then something in the suit's encasing mechanisms kicked into a substantially higher gear and the chill was shunted away. The suit's fabled heat-exchange plumbing had responded. It was like a nightsuit on steroids.

The seabed fell away more rapidly than he had been expecting: nothing that should be insuperable on the return journey, but it was not the shallow even gradient out to the submersible which he had anticipated. He should have used the drone to map the topography. He hadn't thought there was time for that.

Within twenty paces—ten metres? five?—the liquid was pushing against the lower rim of his visor, within another five he was fully immersed and blinded, temporarily, to everything but the HUD's extrapolation of the submersible's location ahead of him. Assuming the gradually diminishing metric was the range, he was now less than a hundred and twenty metres from the stranded vessel. Assuming the quantifier below that value was the depth, he was at three point two metres and still descending slowly. That was a disturbing notion: the suit's density, which assisted the task of walking on the solid but spongily sedimented surface beneath him, meant that he had no hope of attaining the surface above him except by moving to higher (submerged) ground. Buoyancy wasn't a factor considered in lakesuit design, it seemed.

The trail which the HUD had fictionalised for him bottomed out at five point seven metres, considerably deeper than the submersible's location: it must be caught on a sandbar, or something topographically equivalent. He was now climbing gradually towards that, the suit's mass making itself apparent as he did so; likewise the sediment, which was churned by his passage to such an extent that, even at twenty metres' distance, now, from the submersible, he could not get a clear visual on it.

He'd expended ten minutes to reach this point; there wasn't going to be time for anything beyond momentary contact with the submersible before he would need to turn and retrace his steps. Assuming he wasn't cutting it too fine for *that*.

Back at the shoreline, he swapped out the suit's two power units, in sequence, and waited for the chill to abate while he reassessed the situation.

He hadn't been able to establish Portia's status within the vessel; there hadn't been time, and the submersible's viewports were daubed with sediment and, it seemed, condensation. He could wipe off the sediment, but there was nothing he could do about the beads of moisture on the viewports' interior surfaces. He'd merely knocked a few times on the hull; if there had been a response, it hadn't been detectable.

The submersible being lodged on the sandbar presented an opportunity: it was, in principle, possible to propel it, through the exertion of the lakesuit's servos, into the band of deeper liquid between sandbar and shore. It was, in principle, also possible to exploit that depth so as to roll the small single-person craft right side up, like some misshapen barrel. Titan's lake liquid and the suit's own reinforced strength would both help with that. But these actions would require two prerequisites: purchase on an appropriate expanse of seafloor, which he wasn't sure was available; and time, which certainly wasn't. He'd been cautious, in his foray out to the sandbar, but he didn't feel that there was any wisdom in attempting to move faster through an extreme environment with intrinsically unreliable footing. He needed a smarter solution.

To get to and from the sandbar required almost a complete charge of the lakesuit's power units. It wasn't feasible to attempt field repairs on the submersible: he couldn't access anything he would require for that task. The effort required to shift the submersible was, he thought, within the suit's capabilities, but he would be dooming himself in the attempt, and failure to complete it would also very likely doom Portia. He needed to extend the lakesuit's operational duration, and there was only one way to do that. He'd have to find a way to swap out the power units, at least once and possibly twice, while he was out on the sandbar. He couldn't do that while immersed in Kraken; he'd have to climb onto the only solid surface in the vicinity.

He'd need heated rope, as much as he could carry, or chain if any could be found in the Duck's utilities locker. And he would need as many power units as could safely be transported out there in an as yet unidentified sealed container. As plans went, it was extraordinarily rough, and probably desperate; but it was something to work with. He made his way back to the encampment to stock up.

eleven

He'd guided her back towards the encampment. She was mobile, but the makeshift tape repair she'd applied to her helmet's cracked visor had knocked out direct vision, and the HUD's cams were too far askew to correctly knit together a unified binocular view: faced with its eyewatering efforts to display the terrain in front of her, she'd disabled it. She'd asked Cory whether either problem—the taped visor or the disarrayed cams—was something he could straightforwardly repair; his response was noncommittal. There was something he wasn't telling her. Pressed on this, he informed her that the encampment had been sabotaged, and she could tell from his efforts to minimise the incident that he was genuinely fearful. But can the helmet be repaired? she asked.

Cory didn't sound confident that they would have a way to rectify it: helmets were difficult at the best of times, he explained, and the gear they still had on hand was badly depleted after Laith's act of vandalism. Perhaps it would mean that she would need to wear the heavy lakesuit henceforth; perhaps this would mean, in turn, that he would need to be the one to operate the submersible, assuming they could even nurse it back to functionality. His best guess—which had already occurred to Portia, during the ordeal of the past twenty-seven hours—was that sediment, churned during the launch, had been drawn into the lower tanks and had subsequently clogged the methane feed lines. If they could move the submersible to some sort of dry dock, it should be possible to flush the tanks, though the blown propulsor unit on the lower port tank—most likely due to uncontrolled pressurisation beyond the blocked propulsor's failure point—presented a more serious difficulty. Again, with limited tools and equipment, it might be beyond field repair or refabrication.

He didn't know.

She couldn't pilot the submersible without a working helmet. There was always the lakesuit, but it was too bulky for the submersible's minimal-volume airlock.

They reached the encampment. He tried to direct her straight away towards the Duck; she wanted to view the bombing's damage for herself first. She asked him to feed her imagery so she could assess the situation; resistant at first, he complied once she'd insisted.

The wreckage of the outbuilding took her aback: it was difficult to imagine what kind of explosion could disassemble it like that. But the Duck appeared unscathed, which was a relief. She allowed him to steer her towards it; remembered, as an afterthought, the hired trailer. He sent another image, stopped abruptly.

They did not have the encampment to themselves.

twelve

There were two visitors, standing several metres behind the Duck, in T-suits of dull orange-brown which didn't advertise themselves as would the standard visibility-blue casings. Behind them, the spare frames of the single-occupant motorised gliders on which they'd evidently arrived. Laith would be one of them, Cory was sure—his fists attempted to clench within his gloves—with the other presumably the muscle, or the bomber. But he couldn't place which of the pair was Laith.

It transpired neither was.

'Nice lakesuit,' Arum said.

Cory didn't dignify the comment with an immediate response. Instead, he guided Portia towards the Duck's airlock, only belatedly recalling that it was full of paraphernalia. She stayed put, in any event: until he swapped out the lakesuit for his own T-suit, she'd have no usable outerwear. Their helmets weren't compatible, and he was fairly sure his suit wouldn't fit her. He turned to face Arum and the other intruder again. 'You're wasting your time, and Laith's,' he told them.

'Nothing to do with Laith,' said Arum.

'The bombing says otherwise.'

'Even so. We've cut him out. Laith got greedy: he wants the lot, and he wants you dead. We want half, we'll help you reach Westlake so you can stake the claim, and Laith gets nothing. Win-win.'

'Westlake, on those things?' Cory asked, nodding his helmet towards the gliders.

'They'll carry a second over a short distance. That'll get us over to the nearest main island in Hufaidh, and we have a four-person frameplane there.'

'It's moot, anyway,' Cory told her. 'We haven't found anything.'

'Uh, we have,' said Portia.

There was smoke rising from Lulworth. Quite a large column, sunlit along its billowing right side, quite far out. It became apparent when they reached the bend in the streambed, just above the rapids. 'Wait here,' he instructed Portia, then turned and retraced his steps, as hurriedly as the lakesuit would permit, back towards the encampment. Not caring, for the moment, that he'd left her with Arum and the other intruder, not caring that her helmet's vision was shot. Not caring whether Arum would take any measures to oppose his unexplained action.

He'd share his HUD with Portia when he returned, so she could see whatever it was that was occurring. But right now he needed the drone.

Not smoke, he realised when he returned, carrying the drone and its controller. Nor steam, in the conventional sense. A patch of the bay was boiling; what they were seeing was the recondensing hydrocarbon vapour.

Down at the shore, he prepped the drone.

'It's too far out,' Portia told him, when he explained to her what he was doing. 'That's six kilometres out, it has to be. Drone doesn't have the range.'

He didn't waste too much time wondering how she knew the distance. 'It doesn't have the range to return,' he corrected her. 'But it can get very close.'

'You don't have permission to sacrifice it like that,' Portia said, angrier than he could recall having seen her, even about the trailer. She moved in his direction, her voice raised. 'We need the physical artefact of that drone's memory. That is not a point for debate.'

'I have a solution,' Arum said, approaching to stand more or less between them. 'I can carry it out there on the glider, release it when I'm close, retrieve it, bring it back. If you'll give me the controls and clearance to relay the feed.'

'We're wasting time,' said Cory, watching the ongoing eruption behind her. Was this an awakening volcano? Something about the coincidence of timing told him it wasn't.

'Do it,' said Portia, nodding at Arum. Cory turned to her, could find nothing to say.

He had to admit, the motorised glider was faster through the air than the drone would have been under its own flight. The glider was soon so distant that it was only at extreme magnification that his HUD was able to resolve Arum as a recognisable human figure harnessed within the frame of a recognisable aircraft, flying low above the barely troubled liquid shoreward of the towering, funnelling vapour column, in an image which the software struggled to hold steady against the smallest motion of his head.

'Releasing drone. Distance to target two kilometres,' Arum announced in his earpads. 'This thing is big.' She shared the drone's feed with him, and he presumed with Portia and the other T-suited figure. The view was briefly kaleidoscopic, then it stabilised. There was something at the base of the vapour column. But there was also something much larger, a deformity of the sea's surface, briefly visible past the rising cloud of condensing hydrocarbon, past even the heads, through a substantial swathe of Titan's contour-obfuscating haze. A broad dome, rising at what must be thirty or forty kilometres out beyond the drone's position, from the depths of Kraken. The size didn't make sense. None of it made sense.

The drone's attention switched back to the vapour column, then to the emerging structure at its base. The drone moved in slightly closer. Cory had time to formulate the impressions dark and flat surfaces and angular. Then there was a flash, and the feed died. Someone shrieked.

'Arum! Get the hell back,' Cory said, throwing as much urgency as he could into the message. Then there was another flash, a larger one.

A rivulet of molten light seared its way across a gap in the sky, towards the glider. The beginnings of a scream; then silence, save the ringing in his ears. Something small fell unhurriedly into the bay.

'Down,' Portia ordered, and for an instant the word was merely an empty sound, lacking any meaning. Then he saw. The structure, the building-sized dark angular thing from the base of the vapour, was fully airborne now, in a sky which it had briefly shared with the drone, and with Arum.

It was approaching the shore. Fast.

It was almost upon them when they heard the first of the two thunderclaps spawned out on the bay, then the second.

Cory threw himself down flat, no time to care whether he damaged the lakesuit—or himself within it—in the process. Waited for the next flash, the final one.

There was a burst of light, seen peripherally. A detonation, a sense of fragments flung skyward. Close, but not among the trio of prone T-suited figures. He turned his head.

The submersible, a hundred metres or more down the beach, was a shattered shell. Something dark, sharp, large, too fast and too close to characterise more precisely, flew over the ridge. Towards the encampment. He braced, not knowing for what. Within a span that might have been a half-minute at most, the big fast angular shape had reappeared, accelerating back across the sky in the direction of the vapour column. It hit the liquid at the near side of the column's base, vanished in an intensified eruption of cloud. Minutes after, there was a band of heightened wave activity. They got up, moved to higher terrain. The waves subsided.

'Fuck,' said someone. Not Portia. The other woman, still unidentified.

He helped Portia to her feet. Almost stumbled himself in the process, the lakesuit's bulk suddenly unfamiliar to him. There was something wrong with the muscles of his face, and something missing.

Someone.

They cautiously moved back up the streambed, to find out what remained of the encampment.

thirteen

'You weren't to know,' Rosa Xu said. 'None of us had any idea of what to expect.'

'*She* did,' said Cory, the bitterness evident in his tone, even above the rumble of the Duck's drivechain.

Portia, at the controls, could envisage the finger pointed towards her. She bit her tongue, focussed on the driving. It was doubtful anything she could say would help, right now: best that the dialogue was between the two people who'd known Arum well. For herself, she just felt sick; but she didn't have the luxury. It was best to get off Bermoothes.

They'd strapped the one surviving glider, folded, to the Duck's roof. Flight, the need for flight versus the evident danger in getting airborne, was a substantial part of the unease she felt; but whatever had incinerated Arum had descended again beneath Lulworth's surface, and they would just have to hope that the sky west of Bermoothes, the flight path from Hufaidh to Zebker, was unthreatened. There wasn't a choice: the Duck couldn't negotiate the archipelago to reach the mainland, and there wasn't a question of calling in a favour from Junko, not after what had happened out on the bay. Once they'd reached Zebker, there were overland options south, to Yung and then to Toublanc or Sagan, or east to Levin in Cory's case. Her own prospects were a mess; for the moment, the focus needed was on simply staying alive.

There'd be time, in the next few days, to ponder whichever destination would be least problematic for her. The debts would be called in; she couldn't escape that. The grant funding, the trailer hire, the overcapitalisation on the submersible and the supplies they were going to have to mostly leave behind.

The Duck hit a boulder, slewed, slid before it regained traction. Thirty kilometres more of this before they reached Bermoothes' westernmost point; then it would be time to learn whether the glider genuinely could take two at a time.

She turned the cab's heating down another notch. She'd need to keep her wits about her on the drive.

'It spared us,' Cory said; it was almost a complaint. 'Why?'

They'd made it off Bermoothes, were waiting beside the minimally aerodynamic bulk of the frameplane. Rosa Xu had flown back for a third time, to retrieve the empty lakesuit from the Duck; Portia had refused to leave it. 'We weren't a threat,' Portia told him, knowing the words would hurt. There wasn't any helping that.

'She wasn't either. She tried to help us.'

'The structure must've seen it differently.'

'But it—'

'The drone was airborne, and approaching. That made it a threat, to the structure or to whatever it had been placed there to defend. Arum was airborne too, and that was presumably enough. Cory, I'm—'

'The drone, Arum, the submersible. Not us, not the Duck, not the other glider. She… she didn't have a chance.'

'You weren't to know,' she told him. 'I wasn't either, though I knew after that last dive that something was down there. The submersible— probably that thing, the maelstrom, the guardian, the attack craft, whatever you want to call it… it recognised it, after the collision yesterday.'

'But not us,' said Cory, still sounding crestfallen.

'It didn't flag us as a danger. We weren't in the sea, we weren't in the air, we probably weren't the body shape of anything it would recognise as a threat.'

'You still sound like you know what's going on.'

'Really, I don't. All I can do is make a best guess. That's all anyone can do, when there's insufficient data. That thing, that system, was clearly constructed and emplaced as a response to a threat. An autonomous drone, or something like. It came out firing, or at least displaying a readiness to deploy weaponry. Something led up to that point.'

'What, then? If as you say that thing is ancient.'

'It's quite possible we'll never know. But my hunch is this.' She paused to sip somewhat noisily from her suit's water nipple. 'Did you ever hear about 'Oumuamua?'

'No.'

'It was one of the first recognisably interstellar objects, other than comets, to be tracked on its passage through the Solar System, about one and a half centuries ago. It had some odd characteristics: it was substantially elongated, moreso than considered probable in a naturally-occurring object, and its trajectory was changed after perihelion by more than could be expected on purely gravitational grounds. Back then, Earth—and it was only Earth back then—didn't have the pursuit capabilities, and by the time we did, nobody could be bothered. So it wasn't investigated further.'

'I don't see what this has to do with—'

'Like I said, it's just a best guess. There've been other objects since then, also extrasolar, one or two of which we've intercepted on their passage. Those have been natural objects, but what if not all of them are? Most of the Solar System's real estate—Mars, Mercury, the asteroids, any number of moons—are laid bare; two flybys and they're mapped. Most of the rest—Venus, the gas giants—is utterly inimical to anything constructed. Earth? Overrun with animal life. Titan? A conveniently thick obscuring atmosphere, cold, sure, but that can be engineered against. The only problem is that most of Titan is still relatively susceptible to mapping by radar.'

'Why does that matter?'

'What if 'Oumuamua, and/or some of the objects like it, were searching for something as they fell through the System? What if you were what it was searching for? What is the very best place in the System to conceal yourself from something like that? I think it's been in hiding, probably for a very long time. And I woke it yesterday.'

'This still doesn't explain—'

'I don't have more than that,' said Portia, waving as she sighted the returning glider. 'As to what it was guarding, that thing that rose out of Kraken, no idea.'

The frameplane juddered. There was just enough solid surface to it, concentrated at the nose and across the wings, to calm the flow of air around them somewhat, the engines sufficiently powerful to yield unexpected speed in the air. But smooth it was not.

Cory, not a good flier in the best of circumstances, had opted for sedation and an opacified visor, his HUD disabled for the expected seven-hour duration of the flight west and then south towards Zebker. Portia had accordingly piggybacked onto Rosa Xu's HUD; a strange kind of intimacy between people who didn't really know each other. Not that the deal included conversation: Xu appeared to be every bit as taciturn as had been Junko Shaw, which was probably what Portia needed right now. She got to see the terrain ahead, almost as if she was able to see right through Cory's suit in front of her.

Behind her, in the last of the frameplane's four seats, they'd strapped the lakesuit. A hollow placeholder for the one not aboard. *I'll have to emphasise to him, when we get to Zebker or whenever there's an opportunity for dialogue, that it was on my authority that Arum had flown into the maelstrom's path. Otherwise he'll take it on himself.*

'Land ahoy,' said Xu in her earpads. 'That's the end of Hufaidh.'

'West another fifty, I think,' said Portia. 'Give ourselves plenty of distance.'

'Wide berth, yeah,' said Xu, and neither of them said any more after that. It was tempting fate to say they were beyond hazard now; but gradually, as the kilometres from Kraken's western shore accumulated, as the terrain before them and beneath them became hillier, slope after shuffled slope of brown-stained ice with the thin curving and recurving courses of dark braided streams the only liquid interruptions visible upon the landforms, it began to seem that it might be so.

The lakesuit wasn't new, wasn't in the best condition, but it was a good reliable model; she should get a reasonable amount for it in Zebker, enough to arrange repair to her T-suit and a ticket to wherever seemed least problematic. She'd worry about what happened next after that. There were aspects to that thought which were freeing, to a degree, but there was also the dilemma of how to organise her life now that the ambition to honour Prof's research had ended in the way that it had.

The plane commenced banking to the left. It was possibly ghoulish of her to think in this way, but she'd have to ensure she safeguarded the visuals that Arum had transmitted, in the seconds before the end. There'd be detail there which could be analysed, which might yet offer hints to what had occurred. The information would need to be released, to inform appropriate policy about traversing Kraken; or about not traversing it, if the risk of repeated attacks remained. Her hunch was, though, that whatever the guardian had been shielding, it was gone. Though maybe she was as wrong about that as she had been about so much else.

Zebker was a small settlement of several pylon-supported modules connected by enclosed walkways, its elevation seeking both to minimise heat loss to the frozen terrain and to highlight the dark grandeur of the northeast-facing vistas looking towards the southern shore of Kraken's vast southern basin. It was a design which allowed the settlement to cover a larger area than would have a single-shell multistorey hab of the same population, yet to seem smaller, like a village. Portia had passed through it several times before; it was the kind of place that, in a structural sense at least, did not seem to change or evolve measurably between one visit and the next, regardless of the interval between those visits. This time, though, it was crowded.

Rosa Xu had been intending to deliver them to Zebker and then to leave them to whatever outcomes they wished to arrange for themselves. But outbound flights were grounded, and indeed they had been fortunate to have been granted access to land in the first place: Zebker admin were playing it safe, until there was more detail and definition to the shape of the situation in which the northern polar region had unexpectedly found itself.

Portia and Cory booked lodgings, for one night, with the ambition of moving out on the next day if the transportation mavens allowed it. Her finances did not properly permit more than that, and indeed she wasn't sure where she could go. That first night, though, she knew only that after more than two days spent almost entirely in her visually malfunctioning suit, she needed not to feel its confinement around her, its bad air, its infuriating autonomous puffs of scent. She could anticipate the luxury of an honest shower, of a meal not chosen from the limited cuisine of ready-prepareds. She could try to forget, for an hour or two, that terrible flash across the distant sky over Lulworth.

The next day, Zebker's facilities straining with an ongoing influx of the curious, the opportunistic and the otherwise uncategorisable, the settlement also put a temporary hold on inbound travel. There was no visible opportunity for Portia or Cory to depart within the next few daycycles. They were left to pass the time as best they could. For Portia this meant finding out what she could about the events of which they had found themselves on the edge. She sought to interest Cory, too, in this; sought to draw him out of the dark introspection into which he seemed to have fallen. She wanted to help; she did not know how to. The long winter night had fallen again, which would not have helped his mood. This was a time, she knew, when she should say to Cory what she needed to say to him, about her responsibility for Arum's fate; it might be the last such opportunity. But the words wouldn't come together for her.

They met with Rosa Xu, on their second full day in Zebker. Portia invited her to join them, unsure as to whether the idea was sound: as someone to whom he was connected only through Arum, the encounter might be problematic for Cory. But Portia had been growing exhausted of facing his negativism; if there was something which might disrupt him into a less troubled frame of mind, it was worth trying. It at least hadn't made things worse. And Portia had finally felt that she had gained some understanding of the woman: it was difficult to overlook some of the things in which Rosa had been involved in, by association with Laith (and with Arum), but Rosa now seemed to be working hard to put such activities behind her. Of course, it was simpler for her: a wealthy parent, who would need help to get his plan for the foodworks from pipe dream to productivity. It was all a bit too tidy; the prodigal daughter.

'He'll need more than just one more pair of hands, of course,' said Xu, looking meaningfully towards her.

'What are you suggesting?' asked Portia.

'If you find yourself adrift, there'd be work,' replied Rosa. 'That's all.'

Portia hadn't known how to respond. Had only known it wasn't what she wanted, for all that it offered a path leading her from the dilemma she now felt, the need to not get subsumed by the financial and reputational difficulties she would face henceforth. It might also offer an escape from the media attention which would likely follow once someone dragged the name of Wiremu Garrity into whatever had occurred out in Kraken, as was bound to happen sooner or later. Rosa's offer to her was too easy a solution; and she didn't know exactly where she stood with either Xu, father or daughter. She promised to consider the offer, knowing she would not.

There was a chance meeting, also, with Kalpana Braun, the suspended Soderblom pol officer who made a point of hailing Portia on one of the latter's mid-morning forays out into Zebker's main plaza. 'I'm relieved to see you in one piece,' said Braun, without preamble. 'I heard there was a woman killed out there.' She waved vaguely northward.

'There was,' Portia had responded, not trusting herself to offer further explanation. Kalpana Braun was high on the list of people she was wary of; the woman clearly had an agenda. 'So what brings you here?' she asked, seeking to shift the subject off herself.

'Same thing, I think,' said Braun. 'That is to say, an effort to seek to understand what happened out there. Soderblom needs to know if there's any connection with the Ontario Lacus incident. Which, seemingly, there both is and isn't.'

If that had been intended to provoke a clarifying response from Portia, it failed. Instead she asked: 'You've been reinstated?'

'That's still a grey area, moving forward. But let's say that having someone already in the area was too useful a circumstance for Soderblom to overlook.'

'I hope it works out for you.'

'We'll see,' said Braun. 'I'll need to interview both you and Cory, obviously.'

'I think I would prefer to leave that to the local authorities,' said Portia. 'If it has to happen at all.'

'It does,' said Braun. 'Have you reported the death, by the way?'

Portia hadn't. 'I think it's best I leave that to someone who knew her better.' By which she meant Rosa Xu, whom she would now need to contact again; but if Braun interpreted her statement to indicate Cory, she didn't feel inclined to correct that misapprehension. 'If you'll excuse me—'

'Of course,' said Braun, as though they'd been discussing office politics, or the educational development of their children.

Portia returned to the accom unit, not knowing whether to brief Cory on this development. She supposed she would have to.

Information accreted slowly: there had been few direct sightings, even at a substantial distance. It was reported, though, that there had been several fatalities: a lodge owner, wintering over on Mayda Insula, who had announced that he was setting off on a thopter flight, from which he hadn't returned; a mil transport plane, lost near the end of a North Yung to Westlake flight, with either two or five crew depending on which report one gave greater credence to; and a woman on Bermoothes. Arum. Two uncrewed cargo vessels running the Westlake/Mayda ferry service had also been lost. The timing of all of these incidents, allowing for uncertainty, suggested simultaneity, as did satellite imagery of the local tropospheric methane abundance around the fringes of Kraken's north basin: there were abundance spikes in several locations, described by meteorological experts as 'unaccountable by natural processes'.

There was, she thought, something insectile about the whole setup—the suddenly alerted outer defences—but what were they defending? And how and why had the submersible's collision with the Lulworth structure sparked responses at up to five hundred kilometres' distance?

It did not appear that anyone else had footage of anything similar to the structures she and Cory and Rosa Xu had seen: the large dome emerging from Kraken proper; the beweaponed installation which took flight from the base of the funnelling cloud of recondensing methane in Lulworth Sinus. This was perhaps not surprising; nobody else had been searching for anything, and the other air incidents had not had bystanders who had survived. But it meant that the information content in the footage which had been stored in her helmet's memory, and in that of the lakesuit, was invaluable and probably irreplaceable. She would need to ensure that this footage went to those who would most need it, once she'd worked out who that might be.

Her preoccupations were very different to those of most of the people with whom she currently shared Zebker. In the minds (and mouths) of most of those who gave voice to any opinions they might have on the unexplained developments in Kraken, blame was most often attributed to the pharmhands, or the mil. It was far from the first time in the scapegoat role for either group. Denials, of course, changed nothing.

For the moment, the official response was almost as information-poor as the public speculation. It appeared that the mil were currently conducting an extensive program of drone flights and voyages across both northern and southern Kraken, seeking to establish the limits of any no-go zones which would need to be imposed. Any results of this program were not announced to the public. Portia wondered whether that meant they were suffering losses, or whether Kraken's customary cold quietude had reasserted itself.

Zebker, with a suddenly-higher-than-high-summer population and no incoming cargo shipments, began to run problematically low on supplies.

On the sixth daycycle since 'the series of incidents', the ground-transportation ban was annulled, and an exodus began. Rosa Xu contacted them shortly after the embargo's cessation, to inform them that she was travelling out, to Yung and then to Levin and then to Cottini. She had obtained a waiver—doubtless at considerable expense, if Portia's understanding of the situation was correct—to travel not overland but by the frameplane, aboard which there was room. Were she or Cory interested?

Portia was not—she thought she would try to stay on at Zebker, to find those leading the planning for the incident response, and to show them the helmets' captured footage—but she would ask Cory.

Cory just shook his head. Portia didn't push the issue: Arum's, she knew, was still an end which haunted him, and likely the friendship which had existed between Arum and the Xu daughter was a difficult reminder of a relationship which had ended in perhaps the worst way imaginable.

Well, she guessed she knew something of what that felt like. Not that it helped, because he responded negatively to her attempts to extend her condolences or her advice towards him, if he reacted at all. She let him be, since that appeared to be what he wanted. Announced that she was going to track down Zebker's acclaimed marmoset colony, because she needed space and an opportunity to think.

She didn't find the marmosets, and her thoughts merely travelled in circles. There were too many other problems she faced, or refused to face.

She returned to the accom unit disgruntled and angry at herself. She was wasting time, while somewhere there were answers to be had.

Cory, though, seemed brighter. 'Let's have a meal out,' he had said instead. She wondered what had changed for him, in her few hours of absence. 'There's a restaurant I found on the mesh.'

Against her better judgement—her finances were getting perilous—she'd agreed.

Levin, which must have been five times the size of Zebker, was a couple of thousand kilometres distant, east and south. Yet somehow, the restaurant which they found, squeezed between the Zebker Miners' Collective offices and the previously elusive marmoset colony, was an almost identical sibling of the eatery in which they'd first negotiated business between them, five months ago. The lighting, the seating, the not-quite-contemporary decor, even the printcloth napkins and ceramic-look cutlery.

The food was perhaps less diligently prepared; and there was a strange look about Cory, seated across from her. He picked at the meal in his bowl, looked up from it towards her. 'I've been thinking,' he said.

She waited for him to go on.

'I perhaps might need an assistant,' he told her. 'If the repair business in Levin picks up some, it'd be a shame to have to let some of those jobs go because of a staffing deficiency. Which is not to say that I could afford to pay much, to begin with.'

'I—' There was something wrong with her throat. She'd been about to tell him the idea was ludicrous. She sipped at her water, hoping it would help.

'And you're probably about to say that you don't have the expertise. But I've seen you with machines, and I know you're a quick study.'

'We need to talk about Arum,' she said.

'We will. But not here, not now. This is a business meal. So let's stick to that.' He scrawled some details on a napkin, slid it across the table to her. 'Are the terms acceptable to you?'

She glanced at it, succeeded in manoeuvring a morsel onto her utensil, looked back at the napkin, looked up. 'I am not a good business risk right now. My financial situation is in utter disarray, I must have credit demands from Levin trailer hire and all manner of other corps. I should check; I haven't done so. And Braun still wants to interview both of us.'

'All of that can be worked through. I know how methodical you are, how detail-focussed you can be.' He paused to take a mouthful, chewed it thoroughly, swallowed. 'I should also mention that I have some experience in the reinvention of identity, for people who might find that necessary.'

She was struggling as much with the meal as with this conversation. 'I can't ask that of you,' she managed at last.

'You're not,' he explained.

'I would be highly distracted. There's still information I want to extract, to analyse, from the helmets' stored footage. We must be the only people, besides Rosa, who witnessed the thing that emerged from Lulworth, and who saw it at close quarters. And she doesn't have the drone footage. That all needs to be analysed, and I think I need to do that. To help ensure that what… happened to Arum… doesn't happen again, to anyone else.'

'Understood. But you would be doing that on your own time, in between work tasks. Like I say, there would probably be quite a few gaps, until I've managed to build up custom again.'

'I am'—and this part of her thinking process was genuinely new, because she hadn't reached this conclusion previously—'I'm going to need to take this further. The footage, I mean. Even if that construct was autonomous—and I'm guessing it must have been, after how long it must've been down there—it had a capacity for judgment or analysis of some sort, it decided not to attack us. There's scope, therefore, to attempt communication with it. If we leave it to the mil, it'll descend almost inevitably into a confrontation, and how does that help us? Whatever that structure was, we weren't its enemy. We need to convey that message. I need to find a way to convey that message.'

'Whatever you wish to do in your free time would be no concern of your employer,' said Cory. 'The offer stands, and it's sincere, to the extent that the work's available. Do you accept?'

'I'll need time to think about it,' she said. For form's sake. She already knew her answer.

about the author

Born and raised in North Canterbury, New Zealand, Simon Petrie now lives in Canberra, Australia, where he is paid to be careful with words. He has been shortlisted several times for the Sir Julius Vogel, Ditmar, and Aurealis Awards, and has won the Sir Julius Vogel Award three times: in 2010 for Best New Talent and in 2013 and 2018, with *Flight 404* and *Matters Arising from the Identification of the Body* respectively, for Best Novella. He also scored a coveted Dishonourable Mention in the 2011 Bulwer-Lytton Fiction Contest.

He has edited five issues (numbers 35, 40, 51, 54, and 61) of *Andromeda Spaceways Inflight Magazine*, and has co-edited two anthologies (*Light Touch Paper, Stand Clear* and *Use Only As Directed*) with Edwina Harvey and one (*Next*) with Rob Porteous.

A reformed academic, Simon's publishing history also includes numerous studies on the upper-atmosphere chemistry of the Saturnian moon Titan; on the ion/molecule chemistry of the dense interstellar cloud TMC-1 and the circumstellar envelope of the mass-losing carbon-rich post-asymptotic-giant-branch star IRC+10216; on the gas-phase chemistry of multiply charged fullerene ions; and on the structure of the active site of the water-oxidising complex within Photosystem II. He holds actionable views about second person present tense, em-dashes, and Oxford commas.

acknowledgments

There's still much we don't yet know about Saturn's largest, haze-shrouded moon, though the still-ongoing analysis of the wealth of data gathered by the Cassini/Huygens mission continues to augment our knowledge of this fascinating and enigmatic world. In this regard, I must acknowledge the following publications as useful for my fictional extrapolations within this novella:

Brown ME et al. Discovery of Lake-Effect Clouds on Titan. *Geophys Res Lett.* 2009;36:L01103.
doi: https://doi.org/10.1029/2008GL035964.

Cordier D et al. Structure of Titan's Evaporites. *Icarus.* 2016;270:41–56.
doi: https://doi.org/10.1016/j.icarus.2015.12.034.

Farnsworth KK et al. Nitrogen Exsolution and Bubble Formation in Titan's Lakes. *Geophys Res Lett.* 2019;46:13658.
doi: https://doi.org/10.1029/2019GL084792.

Heslar MF et al. Tidal Currents Detected in Kraken Mare Straits from Cassini VIMS Sun Glitter Observations. *Planet Sci J.* 2020;1:35.
doi: https://doi.org/10.3847/PSJ/aba191.

Lorenz RD. The Challenging Depths of Titan's Seas. *J Geophys Res E.* 2021;126:e2020JE006786.
doi: https://doi.org/10.1029/2020JE006786.

Lorenz RD, Mitton J. *Titan Unveiled*. Princeton University Press, 2008.

Lunine JI, Lorenz RD. Rivers, Lakes, Dunes, and Rain: Crustal Processes in Titan's Methane Cycle. *Annu Rev Earth Planet Sci*. 2009;37:299–320. doi: https://doi.org/10.1146/annurev.earth.031208.100142.

MacKenzie SM, Barnes JW. Compositional Similarities and Distinctions between Titan's Evaporitic Terrains. *Astrophys J*. 2016;821:17. doi: https://doi.org/10.3847/0004-637X/821/1/17.

Poggiali V et al. The Bathymetry of Moray Sinus at Titan's Kraken Mare. *J Geophys Res E*. 2020;125:e2020JE006558. doi: https://doi.org/10.1029/2020JE006558.

I am grateful also for the free access afforded to many such publications by the NASA Astrophysics Data System (https://ui.adsabs.harvard.edu/). This is a particularly useful site for those who do not have ready access to the services of a well-resourced university library.

As to the fiction, I'm once again indebted to James Morrison for expertly tidying it up; to Thoraiya Dyer for enthusing; and to the people and cat who share my existence, for putting up with my distractedness while I wrote the thing.

Finally, it should go without saying that any errors, imperfections, etc. in the story are my own work, for which none of the above (except possibly the cat) should be held accountable.

also by this author

Wide Brown Land (stories of Titan)
A collection of eleven hard-SF short stories set on the Solar System's most intriguing moon.
Paperback: 978-0-6483228-2-5
Ebook: 978-0-6483228-3-2

Matters Arising From The Identification Of The Body
Tanja Morgenstein, daughter of a wealthy industrialist and a geochemist, is dead from exposure to Titan's lethal, chilled atmosphere, and Guerline Scarfe must determine why.
(Winner of the 2018 Sir Julius Vogel award for Best Novella.)
Paperback: 978-0-6483228-0-1
Ebook: 978-0-6483228-1-8

Flight 404
The search for the Bougainvillaea brings investigator Charmaine Mertz back to the unwelcoming world of her boyhood.
(Winner of the 2013 Sir Julius Vogel award for Best Novella.)
Paperback: 978-0-6483228-4-9
Ebook: 978-0-6483228-5-6

The 1001 Top Immortality Treatments You Must Try Before You Die
Short fiction, including: the poignant tale of the world's first sentient academic journal; a daring rescue attempt on the searing surface of Venus; a down-on-his-luck would-be assassin caught in a desperate bind; the details now known about Apollo 15's secret fourth astronaut; and a mercifully-short poem written entirely in Webdings.
Paperback: 978-0-6483836-3-5
Ebook: 978-0-6483836-4-2

80,000 Totally Secure Passwords That No Hacker Would Ever Guess
If a collection of unconnected short stories can have (or be) a companion volume, then this is the companion volume to *The 1001 Top Immortality Treatments You Must Try Before You Die.*
Paperback: 978-0-6483228-6-3
Ebook: 978-0-6483228-7-0

Murder On The Zenith Express (the Gordon Mamon collection)
The (now no longer quite complete) adventures of space-hotel employee and reluctant sleuth Gordon Mamon.
Paperback: 978-0-6483228-8-7
Ebook: 978-0-6483228-9-4

Tremendously Inconveniencing A Great Many Photons
An uplifting short novel about pottos, First Contact, and interstellar spaceflight.
Paperback: 978-0-6483836-1-1
Ebook: 978-0-6483836-2-8

www.ingramcontent.com/pod-product-compliance
Lightning Source LLC
Chambersburg PA
CBHW020011140726
47904CB00018B/2228

* 9 7 8 0 6 4 8 3 8 3 6 5 9 *